Nikki Rivers

SEDUCING SPENCER

Harlequin Books

TORONTO • NEW YORK • LONDON
AMSTERDAM • PARIS • SYDNEY • HAMBURG
STOCKHOLM • ATHENS • TOKYO • MILAN
MADRID • WARSAW • BUDAPEST • AUCKLAND

To Ron for believing in love at first sight

ISBN 0-373-16550-1

SEDUCING SPENCER

Copyright © 1994 by Sharon Edwin.

All rights reserved. Except for use in any review, the reproduction or
utilization of this work in whole or in part in any form by any electronic,
mechanical or other means, now known or hereafter invented, including
xerography, photocopying and recording, or in any information storage
or retrieval system, is forbidden without the written permission of the
publisher, Harlequin Enterprises Limited, 225 Duncan Mill Road,
Don Mills, Ontario, Canada M3B 3K9.

All characters in this book have no existence outside the imagination of
the author and have no relation whatsoever to anyone bearing the same
name or names. They are not even distantly inspired by any individual
known or unknown to the author, and all incidents are pure invention.

This edition published by arrangement with Harlequin Enterprises B. V.

® and TM are trademarks of the publisher. Trademarks indicated with
® are registered in the United States Patent and Trademark Office, the
Canadian Trade Marks Office and in other countries.

Printed in U.S.A.

Dear Reader,

This month a new "Rising Star" comes out to shine, as American Romance continues to search the heavens for the best new talent...the best new stories.

Let me introduce you to Nikki Rivers.

Nikki found her first creative outlet in a humor column on teen life called "It's What's Happening, Baby." (No kidding, it was the sixties, okay?) She married young and kept on pursuing her dream of being a writer. After reading her first Harlequin novel, Nikki knew she had found a home for the stories running around in her head. She filched her teenage daughter's electric typewriter and began to pound out her first romance. Nikki lives in Milwaukee with her husband, Ron, the man who taught her to believe in romance, and who helps make *all* her dreams come true.

Turn the page and catch a "Rising Star"!

Sincerely,

Debra Matteucci
Senior Editor & Editorial Coordinator
Harlequin Books
300 East 42nd St., 6th Floor
New York, NY 10017

The white trousers she wore hugged her bottom and the morning sun streamed through them, outlining her long, shapely legs and trim ankles. The woman turned, and Spencer found himself staring at a sheer, tropical print shirt worn over something silky and brief.

The stranger started walking toward him, her hips swaying with her confident stride.

Now *here* was a woman who could take his mind off Georgia. Here was a woman who could take his mind off almost anything.

"Water too cold for a swim this morning?" she asked, and his gaze flew to her face. That voice...

Good Lord—it *was* Georgia.

But not *his* Georgia. This Georgia's skin was somehow brighter, her hair bouncier, her lips fuller, more inviting, her eyes smoky, deeper— eyes he could get lost in.

Eyes he *was* getting lost in.

Chapter One

Georgia Moon never knew what she was going to find when she walked into Spencer Foxworth's house.

"Sorry, Merchant, my conscience wouldn't allow me to design such a house."

She heard the rumble of her boss's voice and realized with relief that he was doing nothing more unconventional than talking on the phone.

Well, the act might be conventional, but the way he looked was decidedly not. Slouched in Georgia's chair, his muscular legs draped in loose, thin cotton that managed to reveal more than the tightest pair of jeans, were stretched out. His feet, in soft leather shoes without socks, were on her desk. Georgia marched over and picked up his feet, rescuing the once tidy stack of papers under them before plopping them unceremoniously to the floor.

Spencer gave her a grin, putting his hand over the receiver. "Just can't keep your hands off me, can you, Georgia?"

"Keep your feet off my desk and I promise to never touch you again."

His eyes sparkling with challenge, he swung his legs back up, stretching his feet across her desk again, blowing her a kiss with lips chiseled by a divine hand.

The man was too damn good looking for his own good. Just under six feet, he wasn't too tall or too short. And his medium frame sported hard muscle that filled him out nicely but didn't leave him overly bulky. He had a long, craggy face, etched with interesting nooks and crannies, including a particularly nice cleft in the center of a square chin. His chestnut hair gave the impression that long, red-tipped fingers had just danced their way across his skull, and his eyes were so dark a blue the color navy came to mind. Or it would, if Georgia ever thought about them.

Which she didn't.

Ten years of close proximity to a man who, for the majority of his thirty-nine years, had played a field of women with all the dexterity and speed with which some men play contact sports, had definitely left her out of the cheering section. Georgia Moon was immune to the Foxworth charms.

"If you want a three-bedroom ranch, any architect will do. Better yet, buy yourself a mobile home," Spencer growled before replacing the receiver with a final-sounding click.

"If that was Kevin Merchant on the phone, you've just annoyed one of the wealthiest men in the Midwest. Your fee for that job would have more than covered what you lost on the last one."

Spencer swung his legs down and stood up. "You worry too much, sweetheart. It'll make you old before your time."

"It's also one of the things you pay me for," Georgia retorted stiffly. "If one of us didn't worry—"

Spencer came up behind her, playfully grabbing the stack of mail she was shuffling through and throwing it on the desk. "If one of us didn't worry, then we'd both be having fun," he finished for her.

Georgia gave him a quelling look and reached for the mail again. She knew what Spencer Foxworth's idea of fun entailed.

One morning, years before, Georgia had found a blonde, gloriously naked, peering over the railing of the loft that served as bedroom. Another morning, showing up for work half an hour early and stepping out onto the patio overlooking Lake Michigan, she'd caught a spectacular view of her boss, just emerging from the waves, sun-glistened water streaming from his body. It took only a moment to realize that he swam without the benefit of a suit. Her back even stiffer than usual, she'd left in too big a hurry to discover which of his many blondes was that morning's companion.

After that, Georgia never arrived early, and she never looked up first thing in the morning.

Turning to place the mail on her desk, she found Spencer there, lounging against it, blocking her way. "Aren't you supposed to be somewhere?"

Spencer laughed. "What's got you so fired up this morning? This May heat wave getting to you, Georgia?" He brought his hands up to straighten the already perfect bow at the throat of the blouse she wore with her conservative business suit. He shook his head, running his hands down her arms. "It's too hot for all these clothes. No wonder you're in such a lousy mood."

"I am not in a lousy mood." She batted his hands away and skirted around him to the other side of the desk.

"Oh, yes you are. And a little nervous, too."

It was true that Spencer Foxworth's house always made her a little nervous. Instead of walls, it had spaces. It had areas. And it had windows. A wall of glass invited a volatile Lake Michigan inside, welcoming the unrelenting light of the sky stretching above it. Regardless of the season or the weather, light, in all its variations, flooded the place.

This particular day was a sunny one, late spring showing off with a vengeance, and Georgia Moon was in no mood for the bright assault. She had the beginnings of a major headache, brought on by the fact that her mother was back, cluttering up her home, cluttering up her life. Jasmine Moon had arrived unannounced only the night before, showing up at Georgia's front door, suitcase in hand. Behind her, drawn up to the curb, a taxi waited ominously, loaded down with Jasmine's nomadic artist's life.

What was more, Georgia's daughter, Emily, had recently shown up at the same front door, having unceremoniously dropped out of college just weeks short of the final semester of her junior year. Emily was showing alarming signs of taking after her grandmother. Georgia figured she was in for one long headache.

But she wasn't about to discuss any of this with Spencer Foxworth. "You'd do well to keep your mind off my nerves and on business," she stated, picking up a legal pad and starting to read from a long list. "The topographical survey for the Hawkins site is in. You can get started on the preliminary sketches. You have that speech to write for the awards ceremony." She tapped a small pile of papers on her desk. "I've made some notes to get you started. And Vinnie called. There's another problem out at the Murdoch site."

She started to go on to the next item on the list, but Spencer put a finger against her mouth, silencing her. "Hold it, sweetheart. That's enough for one morning."

She felt the jolt of his warm finger against her lips. That was another thing that always made her a little nervous—his teasing, his touching. And he knew it. Which was why he did it. Which was why she refused to react like every other red-blooded female in Spencer Foxworth's vicinity. She opened her lips and sunk in her teeth.

"Ouch. Why, you little tigress. I ought to—" Spencer stopped. What ought he do? He could still feel the softness of her mouth around his finger, the slight sting of her teeth. It threw him. Something he definitely wasn't used to.

"You ought to *what?*" she challenged.

Spencer cleared his throat and forced his gaze off her mouth. "I ought to take care of Vinnie first," he said.

Georgia watched him head toward the door with an unhurried, lean-hipped stroll that even a woman who *was* immune couldn't help but admire.

At the door he turned, devil-may-care grin back on his lips, twinkle back in his navy eyes. "Oh, and when Merchant calls back, tell him I won't be free till next week."

"Of all the conceited—" Georgia began, but Spencer just laughed and closed the door behind him.

And the hell of it was, Georgia thought, Merchant probably would call back. Not everyone was suited to live without walls, but after a recent spread in *Architectural Digest,* the Foxworth name was being bandied about in more conservative circles, bringing a sudden flurry of interest.

Georgia checked her calendar for the day, a process she could have easily eliminated as she was much too efficient to forget anything. Whether it was an appointment to interview a prospective client or something as ordinary as picking up Spencer's tux at the cleaners, Georgia was infallible. That done, she picked up a razor-sharp letter opener, making short work of the stack of mail.

Along with the usual bills and advertisements, there were several invitations to speak at conferences and luncheons; Spencer was a favorite with the women's clubs. There was also a letter from a former client gushing on and on about the beauty of life in a Foxworth creation. Georgia always had a hard time understanding the enthusiasm of these dwellers in a wall-less world. She gazed at the wall of glass, following it from the office area, past the sunken living room and on to the kitchen area. So much space. So much light. No, she could never live in such a place. She needed boundaries in her life. She needed structure.

Walking along the wall of windows, Georgia opened a few as she went. Hinged to open inward, they were hung with screens so fine as to be nearly invisible. A fresh lake breeze ruffled her chin-length honey-colored hair and she pushed it back from her face. When she came to the double doors, she pulled them open and stepped out onto the patio, her face lifted to the sun.

The breeze felt cool against her heated body. Spencer was right, it was too warm for such conservative office attire. The gentle, caressing wind made her think of other things—of bare skin and the whisper of short, silky skirts blowing against tanned legs. She had the urge to untie the bow of her blouse and loosen the buttons. She had the urge to throw off the jacket and roll up her sleeves. She had the urge to run through the warm sand, shedding her clothes as she went, and plunging into the cold, cold water, naked—

Georgia gasped and swung her head around as though someone were standing behind her, reading her thoughts. There was no one, but Georgia blushed, anyway. Straightening her jacket and defiantly buttoning it, even though the blush had made her warmer than ever, she hurried inside. See, she thought, that's what living without walls, without boundaries could do to you. Make you think wild, abandoned thoughts. Make you lose control. And above everything in life, Georgia Moon valued her much-guarded self-control.

SPENCER FOXWORTH WASN'T thinking about self-control. Control was something he rarely thought about; it was something he just *did*. It was just there, like the sky or the earth, or the winding road that his low flash of black car ate up. He controlled the car like he controlled everything in his life—effortlessly. Or so it appeared. Or so Spencer Foxworth wanted it to appear.

The car hit the gravel road at too much speed, sending stones popping, stirring up a cloud of dust. He whipped the wheel hard right, fishtailing into the gravel turnaround in front of the site, skidding to a stop just inches from the man who stood there. Spencer laughed heartily. He liked a good entrance.

Vincent Prescott didn't move a muscle. Whether it was trust in the man or trust in the car that made him stand his ground, was hard to say. From the look of the compact frame encased in worn jeans and a ragged flannel shirt, more gone than there and showing plenty of hard, tanned muscle, it could simply have been stubborn male pride that kept him from flinching.

Brown eyes squinting, a mocking tilt to his mouth, Vinnie peered through the gray haze of dust the Jag had kicked up. "Hey, Foxworth! You sure like to make your presence felt." He coughed, shaking dust from his dark hair. "Damn shame, you know," he muttered mournfully, running his hand lovingly along the hood of the Jag, "treating her the way you do. Yup, damn shame."

Spencer held his hand against the sun, gazing at the structure he had designed. It was taking shape now, giving broader hints of what it would become. An exciting time for an architect, excitement Spencer felt the need to conceal. Spencer Foxworth might have done away with walls in his house, but there were some invisible ones he'd built years ago that didn't come down so easily. Vinnie Prescott had been the contractor on other Foxworth projects and he knew him well enough to like him as a man, but there were some things he didn't share with anyone.

Keeping the moment light, Spencer grinned recklessly. "I save my TLC for my women, Vin. No sense wasting it on a hunk of fiberglass you can pay someone else to wash."

Vinnie laughed. "Can't argue with you there, Spence. I'd rather give one of your ladies a bath any day."

Spencer shook his head. "Come on, Vin, you know you're a one-woman man."

"Yeah, guess you're right about that. Trouble is, at the moment I'm a no-woman man."

Spencer shrugged. "You'll get over Carol leaving, your heart will mend, you'll find someone else."

"Easy for you to say, Foxworth. Hell, you never have to go looking, you just sit there and they come begging."

Spencer laughed. Well, not all of them, he thought. Not Ms. Georgia Moon. Which was just as well, he hurried to add. A woman like Ms. Moon had too many walls for a man like Spencer Foxworth. "Come on," he said, getting his mind back on business. "Show me the latest little fiasco on this project."

The two men spent some time over blueprints and sketches. When they had the problem solved, Spencer did his usual inspection of the work in progress, joking with some of the men he had worked with before. Prescott Builders was owned and operated by Vincent Prescott from a crowded desk in the living room of the house he was remodeling for himself, and from the back of an old panel truck. He was young, only thirty, but he was good. The kind of contractor with a feel for wood, the kind who got dirty right alongside of his men. It was the reason he inspired such loyalty in men nearly twice his age, and the reason Spencer handed out Vinnie's business card to clients looking for a contractor.

After a shared sub sandwich and a quick game of poker with the guys, Spence headed out toward the rolling hills near Kettle Moraine State Forest to check out two possible sites for a client. He spent some time walking the terrain, finding one site as beautiful as the other. In the end he made up his mind to recommend the second site for its hill overlooking the narrow winding roads, checkered farmland and lush green forest. Spence could easily picture designing a home for the spot, the wall of glass he couldn't seem to do without giving a spectacular view in any season.

By the time he pulled into his own driveway, the sun was sinking in the west and the house was empty.

He tried to get down to work on the preliminary sketches for the Hawkins site, but he couldn't find the topographical survey. He rummaged through Georgia's desk top to no avail, opened her file cabinet and flipped through the neatly ordered files, finding nothing. Her desk drawers were locked. He rattled the knobs, convinced that what he needed was inside, just out of his reach.

Why wasn't she here when he needed her? He was used to saying, "Georgia, where is this? Georgia, could you get me that?" It embarrassed him to admit it, but he didn't know his way around the office portion of his own home.

Hell, why should that embarrass him? That's why he had Georgia, wasn't it? He was the creative end; she was the business end. All business, usually. So why wasn't the topographical survey out in plain sight? She should have known he'd want to start on it tonight.

Picking up the phone, he started to dial her home number, then thought better of it. He'd just drive over there, pick up the desk keys and save himself the lecture he'd get if she had to drive back out here with them. Besides, in ten years, he'd never been to her house. Maybe he was getting a little curious.

THE INCESSANT BUZZ and thump of industrial rock music hit Georgia as she let herself into the tiny Cape Cod in one of Milwaukee's older suburbs. She looked up at the ceiling and swore she could see the plaster vibrating.

"Emily!" she called up the stairs. "Emily!" she repeated somewhat louder. But it was impossible to be heard above the technoracket.

"Georgia—"

Georgia nearly jumped out of her skin. Hand on her heart, she swung around. "Mother, please don't sneak up on me like that. Honestly, you could give someone a heart attack." Her gaze followed the flowing line of the gauzy caftan floating around her mother's tiny frame, to the perfect little toes peeking from the lavender fabric. "Honestly, Mother, don't you ever wear shoes?"

Her mother smiled that placid smile Georgia always found so irritating, her green eyes shining with the serene humor she so often found in life. "Would you like me to wear a bell around my neck, George? On the other hand, if you took the herbal preparations I've concocted for you every day maybe you wouldn't be so uptight, love."

On her way to the living room, Georgia kicked at one of the cartons piled in the minuscule entrance hall, which was made even smaller by the cluttered country look currently in decorating vogue. "And perhaps," she stated, "I wouldn't be so uptight if I didn't have to maneuver through your junk when I walk in the door at night." A particularly loud crescendo echoed from the upper floor and Georgia's eyes shifted ceilingward, a grimace marring her mouth. "Or have to shout to be heard over that—that—"

"It's Nitzer Ebb," her mother supplied matter-of-factly. "And there's no place else to put my belongings. You've filled every nook and cranny of this unimaginative hovel with things that are ruffled or have Welcome painted on them."

Georgia bristled inwardly at her mother's description of her home. The place was her sanctuary and she had filled it to overflowing with the comforts and furbelows of what she had always considered a home to be. To Georgia it was the symbol of the constancy and stability she'd never had in her life. When she'd bought it, she'd been desperate to put down roots, roots her early marriage was supposed to have given her, but hadn't. In that it had failed miserably. In fact, in just about every aspect it had failed. All but one. It had given her Emily. And Emily had always been a delightful child—that is, up until a few weeks ago.

Jasmine reached up and patted her daughter's cheek. "Don't worry, love, my stay is temporary, as I told you. As soon as I find a place—"

"Oh, Mother." Georgia sighed. She didn't like fighting with her mother, really she didn't—especially since her mother rarely fought back. She just was no good at these upheavals. She had enough of them, thank you, working as Spencer Foxworth's assistant. She counted on home to be quiet, predictable. "You're welcome to stay here, really you are. It's just that—"

Jasmine patted Georgia's cheek again. "I know, love. It's just that I'm invading your space."

Georgia grimaced again. "Well, I wouldn't have exactly put it that way, but—"

"I know, love, but you shall have your space back before you know it. An artist friend of mine told me about an abandoned barn that—"

"An abandoned barn? Really, Mother."

"Well, what did you expect? An off-white apartment in a retirement community? George, I need room for my canvases and my loom and—"

The doorbell chimed.

"You look tired, George. Want me to get that?"

Georgia's sigh was heavier this time. "No, I'll get it." She started to maneuver through the cardboard maze. "And don't call me George," she threw over her shoulder just as she threw open the door.

"Okay, okay." Spencer Foxworth stood on Georgia's front stoop, hands raised, mocking grin on his face, loose cotton shirt unbuttoned low enough to allow a tantalizing glimpse of dark chest hair. "Don't shoot. I surrender completely. Ms. Moon it is."

Georgia's mouth dropped open. Spencer Foxworth had never been to her house before, and she couldn't figure out what he was doing here now.

"What—?" Georgia began but Spencer wasn't paying attention. Instead he pushed past her, looking around in bemusement, as though he'd never seen a normal house before.

He stood on the threshold of the living room shaking his head, his glance going from the authentic antique spinning wheel in the corner, to the excessively ruffled curtains at the window, to the dry sink—a reproduction this time; she couldn't afford the original—with its cascading English ivy, to the chintz-covered sofa scattered with what looked like dozens of needlepoint throw pillows. "This is amazing," he finally said.

Georgia peered over his shoulder, trying to figure out what he could possibly find amazing in her living room. It looked perfectly normal to her. "What?" she asked.

"Your home is even more oppressive than your wardrobe." He turned to look at her. She was closer than he'd thought, and he found himself staring directly into her big, baffled eyes. He felt a direct hit in his gut. The house might be overdone, but it was also feminine. A side of Georgia she kept successfully hidden. His mind started to wander uncharted territory as his eyes wandered over her conservative clothes. He couldn't keep himself from imagining what was beneath it all—just like he imagined what her living room would look like stripped bare.

Georgia frowned. She didn't like the way his eyes were moving over her, didn't like the way it made her feel. Weak and defensive at the same time. She clamped down on the weakness and came out fighting. "The decor is country, Spencer," she huffed.

"The decor is stifling, Georgia. You've taken a small, potentially charming room and suffocated it." His hand came out to tug at the bow at her throat. "Just the way these clothes must be suffocating you."

The bow easily came undone in his fingers. She felt the give at her throat, felt the cooler air of the room hit her damp skin. She looked down at his tanned fingers, still holding the length of fabric.

"You ought to let it breathe," he murmured.

Her eyes left his fingers and moved up to his face. "Let it breathe?" she croaked, finding it a little hard to.

"Tear down those curtains, give the room light and air. Rip away—"

Georgia swallowed. "Rip away?" she murmured in a voice made a little breathless by the blue intensity of his eyes.

Spencer watched her lips form the word *rip,* pursing then parting. He cleared his throat and ran a hand through his hair, turning back to the living room. "The carpeting—you should rip away the carpeting."

Yes, of course, Georgia thought. He was talking about the room. Where on earth had her mind been wandering? She retied her blouse.

"My guess is you'd find a solid oak floor underneath. It would give the room an aura of space. And all these ruffles and pillows—"

"Hey, I made those pillows myself. They're beautiful."

Spencer picked one up, squinting at the delicate stitchery, then turning his navy-blue gaze back on her. His brow rose; his voice lowered. "This is what you do with your nights?"

Georgia looked at his strong hands holding the pillow, the contrast of his long, tanned fingers against the delicate pink of the needlepoint flowers. Before she could let herself imagine what those hands did with their nights, she snatched the pillow away from him. "Yes, it is," she replied testily, "and it's certainly a lot more wholesome than what you do with yours."

She replaced the pillow in its appropriate spot, smoothing the ruffle on the arm of the sofa. "And I could never get rid of my pillows or my ruffles or—or my curtains. Why, I'd feel—I'd feel exposed!"

Spencer's eyes moved insolently down her body, an illegal smile twitching one corner of his mouth. "That's the idea, George," he said in a low rumble. "Get down to the bare necessities and find out who you really are."

"A man after my own heart," came a voice from the corner.

Georgia groaned, wishing she could just go on forgetting there was anyone else in the room. The expectant look on Spencer's face made that impossible and she turned to face the inevitable. "Spencer Foxworth," she said, "meet my mother."

OF COURSE HER MOTHER had offered Spencer iced herbal tea, and of course there wasn't any made. Georgia, drumming her fingers on the kitchen counter, waited for the kettle to boil. She didn't like the idea of Spencer and her mother sitting on her oppressive sofa, discussing her. She didn't like it at all.

For ten years she'd managed to keep Spencer, and his philosophy of life, out of her private life. Her mother, whom she suspected was here largely to back Emily's decision to drop out of college, was enough to handle. The last thing she needed was Spencer Foxworth dropping in unexpectedly for little visits. The last thing she needed was to feel confused and fluttery, like some naive schoolgirl, when he teased her. He always teased her. She was used to it—or thought she was. Of course, he'd never teased her in her own living room before, surrounded by the trappings of her ordered but solitary life. She had been right to keep him away from her home. And just as soon as he gulped his glass of herbal tea, she was getting him out of there.

The kettle finally whistled. "About time," she muttered, throwing tea bags and ice into a pitcher. By now her mother probably had Spencer on the sofa next to her, teaching him to meditate or offering to whip up a potion of herbs to stimulate his mind and body—clearly not an area Spencer Foxworth needed help with.

Standing in the doorway with the loaded tea tray, Georgia watched the couple on the sofa in animated conversation. At sixty-five, her mother still possessed the delicate beauty of her youth. The tiny lines around her eyes detracted very little from the fine, porcelain quality of her skin and the silver streaking her hair only served to highlight the pale blond color. She moved with subtle grace, keeping her small, fine-boned body trim and supple with yoga and hiking.

Georgia sighed, feeling even larger than usual in her big-boned, five-foot-nine frame. Trust her luck to take after her father....

Spencer was aware of her coming back into the room. He watched her bend down to put the tray on the coffee table, watched her look nervously up at him, then just as quickly look away. She'd retied the bow on her blouse, tight as ever, but there was something a little flushed in her cheeks, something a little soft around her mouth. He'd gotten to her— he'd be willing to bet on it. He settled a few of her ruffled pillows at his back and settled in for a nice long visit. This new side of the prim Georgia Moon was definitely worth exploring.

"George, you never told me your mother was Jasmine Moon, the artist."

"Didn't I?" Georgia asked with an air of innocence.

"And she never told *me* that her boss was such a handsome, charming man," replied Jasmine.

Georgia watched her boss and her mother beaming at each other and muttered, "Oh, brother."

True to form, Spencer had flirted with Georgia, then moved on to the next available female without a backward glance.

And why not? thought Georgia. Jasmine was exactly his type—small, blond, completely feminine and totally independent.

The music from above suddenly stopped, throwing Georgia off balance for a second before she settled back in her chair with a sigh of relief. "Thank God. I don't know how she can stand listening to that stuff."

Spencer turned his smile her way. "What stuff?"

"That music! Surely you heard it?"

He shook his head. "Didn't hear a thing." His attention returned to Jasmine. "But, then, I'm always a little single-minded when I'm talking to a beautiful, fascinating woman."

Georgia wanted to throw up, but Jasmine was looking at him like she believed every silly word. Georgia had had enough. She was tired. She was hot. She wanted to step under a cold shower and try to forget that in a remarkably short time her life had become much too complicated.

"Spencer, what are you doing here, anyway?"

"Ahh. . . ." Spencer looked blank, but only for a fraction of a second. "The topographical survey for the Hawkins site. I couldn't find it anywhere and I need it if I'm going to start on those preliminary sketches. I looked all over—on your desk, in your files. I figured it was probably locked in a desk drawer so I came over for the key."

Georgia looked skeptical. "Did you try looking on your worktable?"

He stood up, shoving hands into his pockets, leaning forward from the waist and giving her that little smile that deepened the grooves running down his cheeks. The one that raised one bushy brow about a half inch. The one Georgia was immune to. "Well, of course I looked on my worktable, Georgia. That's the first place I'd look."

She peered up at him, wondering why he was wasting all this charm on her. She almost suspected that he was here for some other reason. That he was here because he wanted to see her. Nonsense—flirting with women was as unconscious an act as breathing to the man. She just happened to be handy at the moment. "If that's true," she finally answered with exaggerated sweetness, "then you would have found it, because that's exactly where I put it before I left."

He looked a little confused. "Really? Hmm—I thought I looked—" Then he grinned at her. "Guess I should have known that the efficient Ms. Moon would have placed the survey exactly where it should be."

"Just one of George's many compulsions, Mr. Foxworth," Jasmine supplied sweetly.

Spencer looked Georgia up and down, brow still quirked. "Oh? And what else is she compulsive about?'' he asked, his voice a lazy, suggestive rumble.

Georgia blushed. She had a sudden flash of something not altogether nice—not for present company, anyway. She thought back to the episode on Spencer's patio that morning. It was the second time that day that her thoughts had been decidedly un-Georgia-like.

She glanced worriedly at her mother. The woman had only been here overnight. Was she corrupting her already?

Spencer's attention was suddenly drawn to something behind her. Georgia turned to find her daughter descending the stairs, legs first. And quite a sight it was, too. Emily was a younger version of her grandmother, small and delicate. But her legs, going on forever till they reached the edge of her miniskirt, managed to give the illusion of length. She seemed to be walking in slow motion, Georgia thought irritably with a glance at Spencer's narrowed, expectant gaze.

When the rest of Emily finally did emerge, the effect was even worse. Her recently shorn blond hair framed her delicately featured face. An oversize cotton sweater, negligently hanging off one pale, creamy shoulder, was a shade calculated to bring out the startling green of her eyes—eyes that were now alight with a good deal of interest in Spencer Foxworth.

Chapter Two

Any female would have a hard time not noticing the extreme hunkiness of a man like Spencer Foxworth. But Emily Moon was not just any female. She was Georgia's daughter, and Georgia expected her to have more sense than to notice.

Emily paused only for a moment, the smile on her lovely mouth widening ever so slightly, before she gracefully descended the rest of the way down the stairs. She held out her hand.

"You're Spencer Foxworth," she said. "You were in *Architectural Digest* a few months ago. The pictures were wonderful. I'm Emily Moon and I'm so happy to meet you."

Spencer took the offered hand, placing his other hand over it and holding on much longer than a mere introduction warranted. "Well, well," he said, "George's little girl seems to have grown up quite nicely."

"Thank you," Emily said straight into those navy-blue eyes.

Emily took after her grandmother in more than just looks. She was conveying the same air of unwavering interest that Jasmine always showed men. Georgia felt a wave of uneasiness. Emily was beautiful, smart, graceful and showing alarming signs of independence. And at twenty, she was not all that much younger than the average Foxworth lady. She was a perfect candidate.

An alarm sounded in Georgia's head. Her back stiffened and she went into action. "Mr. Foxworth is just here about some papers. I may have a copy in my briefcase, Spencer. I'll go take a look. I'm sure you'd like to be on your way."

"No hurry, Georgia. I just got here."

The words reached Georgia on the way to her briefcase in the front hall, hitting her with another wave of uneasiness. How long did he plan to stay?

The copy of the topographical survey wasn't hard to locate, and she was only gone a minute, but even so, Spencer and Emily were already clearly making a connection by the time she returned.

"It must be exciting to see something you've designed on paper become a reality. I'd love to visit a site sometime during construction—see the prints, watch the house take shape."

Georgia would have liked it better if Emily had giggled and blushed. But Emily was no longer a girl—she was a woman. In fact, she was so poised, so perfect, that Georgia knew she should be admiring her daughter. And she would be—if Spencer Foxworth wasn't so busy doing that very thing.

Before Georgia could prevent it, her boss was inviting her daughter out to the Hawkins site.

"Here." She thrust the folder of papers at him, took his arm and steered him toward the door. "You must be in a hurry. Sorry it took so long. Have a nice night—"

She was shutting the door in his face when he called out, "Bye, Emily. See you tomorrow morning—"

SPENCER SMILED to himself as he got into his car. Imagine Georgia having such a beauty for a daughter. Then he thought, Well, why not? Georgia was beautiful, too. But the girl got her looks from her grandmother. They were both small, delicate, lovely. Georgia—Georgia was all woman, and almost as tall as he was. The kind of woman that in another day would be referred to as strapping. Definitely not delicate.

Vibrant—that was the word for Georgia. She pulsed with vibrant energy—even her skin glowed with it. No, not delicate—but soft. Maybe the softest-looking woman he'd ever known. But Spencer knew that beneath all that softness was a spine of steel and plenty of well-honed hard edges.

She had made it clear very early in their association that she was a no-nonsense woman who had no room in her life for a man—especially him. She'd done such a damn good job of keeping him out of her personal life that this was the first time in ten years he'd ever been to her home. And, boy, had she not wanted him there! She couldn't get him out the door fast enough.

Spencer started the car and eased thoughtfully away from the curb. By the time he rounded the corner, he was grinning and shaking his head. Georgia Moon might be a no-nonsense woman, but something about having him in her living room sure made her nervous.

FOR THE FIRST TIME in ten years Georgia wasn't alone on her way to work. Emily, looking morning-fresh in tight jeans and light cotton sweater, sat beside her in the car, singing softly along with the radio, oblivious to the distress in her mother's heart.

Watching her nice, safe suburb recede in the rearview mirror, Georgia felt she was crossing an invisible line—the boundary between her personal and professional life. Once her daughter entered the unnatural abode of Spencer Foxworth, nothing would ever be the same again. She was sure of it.

"It's beautiful out here, isn't it?"

Georgia glanced at her daughter, whose short cap of hair was tousled by the wind, happy expectancy lighting her face. Feeling like she was leading a lamb to slaughter, Georgia forced her eyes back to the winding road.

Yes, Georgia supposed, it was beautiful. The narrow road followed the twists and turns of the shoreline, only yards away. The water, in its sun-dappled morning glory, chopped gently toward shore. Gulls swooped and cried, fishing for breakfast, riding the currents of air that felt fresher, smelled purer, than those they'd left behind.

"Have you thought at all about going back to school?" As soon as it was out, Georgia knew it was the wrong thing to say.

Emily gave a disgusted snort. "What is it with mothers, huh? Do they give classes on how to ruin a moment immediately after you give birth? I can just see it—millions of mothers being wheeled from the delivery room directly to this huge seminar where they learn how to ask questions like that at moments like this."

"All I asked was—"

"Yeah, Mom, I know what you asked. And no, I haven't, as in no, I'm not going to. I told you when I came home last week that this was it—I've had it with school. If I'm serious about being an artist, I'd just be wasting *my* time, and *your* money, finishing school."

"But a degree in art education would—"

"Give me something to fall back on," Emily finished for her. "Mom, I don't want to teach, I want to *do*. Jasmine didn't waste time going to school and she's had a perfectly decent life with her art."

"You might gain greater insight into that life by asking her daughter about it."

"You just don't appreciate the freedom you were raised with." Emily settled herself pointedly against the back of the car seat, folding her arms across her chest. "Honestly, I should have been Jasmine's daughter. She understands my choices perfectly. And," Emily added defiantly, "she thinks I have talent."

"Emily, a few pieces of sculpture isn't a lot to base a career decision on."

"Exactly. That's why I quit school. Try to understand, Mom. I've got to give it a shot—and now is the time."

"But—"

"I've made up my mind, so just drop it, okay?"

So Georgia dropped it, the distress in her heart moving over to make room for a little hurt. Every conversation since Emily came home turned into a battle, and now that Jasmine had been called in to beef up the opposition, the real war was about to begin. The irony was that although Georgia knew in her heart she couldn't win, something kept her in there fighting just the same. Another mommy tactic learned in that giant seminar Emily had conjured up?

Suddenly, Emily sat up straighter, leaning forward, her excitement almost palpable in the small car. "Is that it?" she asked, her voice once again brimming with enthusiasm.

"That's it," Georgia conceded, turning the car into the drive.

Spencer Foxworth's house stood alone on a narrow peninsula of land jutting into Lake Michigan. The road, only a few miles out of Milwaukee's North Shore suburbs, was hardly deserted, but the house had the good fortune to be one of the few on the lake side and had no immediate neighbors, giving the setting a certain remoteness while still being in close proximity to the city.

In the Usonian tradition of Frank Lloyd Wright, the house turned its back on the road. To the passerby it was a plain, white concrete structure, curving into a crescent. The house came alive on the lake side, the inward curve of the wall of windows, rising from floor nearly to ceiling, reflecting the water, embracing the lake, making it part of life.

As soon as Georgia parked the car, Emily bounded out, her artist's heart drawn like a magnet to the smooth, unblemished concrete.

"It's magnificent—unbelievable. The ultimate functional sculpture—"

Georgia couldn't see it. Oh, she would admit that the lake side of the house had certain qualities that some people might admire, but the starkness of this side of the house always threw her. It sat on the land like it wasn't a part of it—like it would never be a part of it. Emily was right. It did look like sculpture, the modern kind whose form gave no clue as to what it represented, and whose name even less. The kind Georgia had always hated. The kind Emily wanted to spend her life creating. The kind Spencer Foxworth and Emily Moon could probably talk about for hours.

It just didn't bear thinking about.

By the time Georgia made her way inside, Emily was already getting the grand tour.

Georgia winced at the long, brown fingers lightly resting on Emily's shoulder, steering her from goody to goody, while she gushed enthusiastically about how wonderful, how free, life must be in this marvelous wall-less creation.

"*Architectural Digest* didn't do it justice, Mr. Foxworth."

"Please, call me Spencer," that man smoothly said as he guided Emily up the staircase toward the loft—toward the bed.

Georgia's heart nearly stopped. Up they went slowly, talking, Spencer's very masculine hand still resting on Emily's pink knit shoulder. It was the image that had kept her tossing and turning the night before, seeking an elusive sleep. It was the image she'd seen in her dreams, indelibly embedded in her mind upon waking that morning. Her worst nightmare come true.

Of course, she knew nothing was going to happen with her standing there. Probably nothing would happen for quite some time yet. First there would be intimate lunches in trendy little places, progressing to dinners out. Then dinners in, before a roaring fire in the circular, freestanding fireplace. Then walks on the moonlit beach, the final seduction accompanied by the sound of waves lapping the shore.

She knew the routine. She'd seen it performed dozens of times in the last ten years, but she'd be damned if she would see it performed on her daughter!

She looked up at the loft but couldn't see what they were doing up there. How long could it take to look at an eighteen-by-twenty-foot *space?* They were certainly taking their time. Georgia was just starting for the stairs when the phone rang. She glanced back at it, torn. In the end she gave up and returned to the desk to answer it. It was, after all, what she was there for.

Georgia bit her lip at the sound of Eloise Hawkins's voice. "Yes, Mrs. Hawkins. He started on the preliminary sketches last night.... Of course, Mrs. Hawkins.... Well, he's planning on going out to the site this morning. In fact . . . No, that's quite all right, Mrs. Hawkins, he understands how excited you are. . . . Yes, I'm sure he will. . . ."

Emily and Spencer finally started down the stairs, and Georgia put her hand over the receiver. Once Eloise Hawkins got started, she'd never know Georgia was missing.

"It's Eloise Hawkins. It seems she and Arthur were up half the night discussing closets and bookcases. She can't wait to talk to you."

But Spencer was shaking his head and steering Emily toward the front door. "Tell her I've already left."

"But—"

"Just take notes, Georgia. You know what to do."

"Bye, Mom." Emily waved, and out the door they went.

SPENCER TOOK THE GRAVEL road at a much slower pace than the day before. For some reason he felt very protective toward Georgia Moon's daughter. Emily had loved the site for the Hawkins home, showing awed enthusiasm at getting the first look at the parti—the rough sketches of the project. Now he thought she might like viewing a project already underway. Truth was, he liked basking in her youthful admiration and respect—two things he'd never gotten from her mother.

He left Emily waiting at the car and went in search of Vinnie, finding him two stories up, balancing on a plank. "Hey, Vin, cut the high-wire act. You've got company."

Vinnie squinted down at him, then swung his gaze toward the Jag, shaking his head in wonder. "Looks like you did it again, good buddy. That is one beautiful girl. Where did you find her?"

"Believe it or not, I found her on Georgia Moon's doorstep. Emily is Georgia's daughter."

"You're kidding, right? I mean, there's no way Georgia Moon is going to let an old reprobate like you date her daughter."

Spence shook his head. "It's not a date, Vin. The kid just wanted to see a working site. She's properly in awe of my genius—which is more than can be said of her mother. Come down off your perch and I'll introduce you."

"WHAT MADE YOU BECOME an architect?" Emily asked over a late lunch of spinach fettuccine at a little pasta place on Milwaukee's east side.

She had her mother's skin, thought Spencer. Pale and fine, tinged with a glow of pink across her cheekbones. And she had beautiful eyes, a pure and shining green. And she was eager—very eager. Sitting there with her chin propped prettily in her hand, she knew exactly what she was doing—getting him to talk about himself. That's what all these young, pretty girls did.

How many pretty young girls had he sat over lunch with? Too many to count. And yet in two months he would turn forty, and there was no one in his life who would even care. When he came to the Midwest he had been only thirty and the girls had been the same age as Emily was now. He had gotten older but the girls never had—not much older, anyway. Spencer liked them young and independent, the kind that would spend a pleasant interlude with him, then go their own way; the kind that wanted commitment and involvement even less than he did. And because he had never wanted anyone to have a hold over him, have any say in how he lived his life, he was going to end up alone.

Emily was still waiting for an answer, so he gave it to her. "I wanted to create places where people could live in freedom and harmony, places without walls and boundaries."

"You're very talented," she said, then rolled her eyes in self-mockery. "Like you really need me to tell you that."

"It's always nice to hear, and I thank you. Actually, though, I'm not everything an architect should be. A good architect subordinates the projection of his own personality when he designs. I'm afraid I'm not very good at that. So far, I haven't been able to get away from the concept of a house without walls." His mouth quirked wryly. "Your mother often points out all the commissions I'm losing out on."

"My mother has trouble understanding the artistic temperament," Emily moaned.

Spencer raised a brow at that. "Oh? Trouble on the home front?"

Emily shrugged. "I dropped out of college to concentrate on my sculpting and, of course, Mom doesn't understand." Emily wrinkled her nose and toyed with her pasta. "Mom's so staid and set in her ways—she has no passion in her, so how can she understand an artist's passion for his work?"

"Georgia may be set in her ways, but I'd hardly call her staid or passionless." Spencer thought for a moment, conjuring up an image of Georgia in his mind. He grinned to himself, picturing her over the years, taking him on when she thought he was wrong, taking his clients on when she thought he was right. Many a time her temper and passion had livened his solitary existence. "When I think of your mother," he said with something almost wistful in his voice, "the word *feisty* comes to mind."

Emily gave him a long look. "Really? Hmm, that's interesting. I guess Mom's a fighter, if that's what you mean."

"That's putting it mildly. The woman would start World War Three if it got her what she wanted."

Emily laughed. "Well, the house has been a war zone since I got home. Guess I'm in for a long haul, hmm?"

"Stick to your guns, kid. Everybody's got to do what they've got to do. But that includes your mother, so go easy on her."

Emily grinned. "You like her, huh?"

Now it was Spencer who shrugged. "Sure, I like her."

"No, I mean you *like* her."

"Listen, kid, ten years ago when your mother first came to work for me, I made a pass and nearly lost my life for it. If I tried anything again she'd scream sexual harassment so fast I wouldn't know what hit me."

"Sounds like Mom," Emily conceded. "But you still haven't answered my question."

"Yeah? Well, like every kid, you ask too many." Emily looked amused enough for him to ask, "What?"

"Just the way you keep calling me 'kid.' What happened to your reputation as a womanizer? You sure didn't get all those young girls I've heard rumors about with this daddy routine."

Spence chuckled softly and shook his head. Another thing Emily Moon obviously got from her mother was her directness. She plunged right in and said what was on her mind same as Georgia did. "No, you're right, I didn't. I guess people change."

"Everybody but my mother," Emily groaned. "But enough about her," she said, her voice back to its usual brightness as she wiggled in her chair. "Tell me all about Vinnie Prescott."

Spencer threw back his head and laughed.

GEORGIA LOOKED AT her watch—again. It was nearly six o'clock. She should have left for home almost an hour ago. Where on earth were they?

She was pacing to the wall of windows for the hundredth time when she heard the sound of the front door opening behind her.

"Georgia—what are you still doing here?"

"What am I doing here? Where have you two—" She swung to face him and found out he was alone. "Where's Emily?" she demanded, her overactive maternal imagination conjuring up all sorts of lurid possibilities.

"Home," Spencer answered.

That took the wind out of her a little. "Home?" she repeated.

"Yeah. I thought you'd be gone for the day, so I dropped her off."

"Oh." What could Georgia say to that? Of course, it still didn't explain where they'd been all day. She'd been left to field calls from an increasingly irate Eloise Hawkins while Spencer had Emily in his clutches, filling her head with heaven only knew what. "Where have you been all day?"

"Well, first I took Emily out to the Hawkins site, then we went to the Murdochs. She seemed fascinated by the whole process—"

"I'll just bet," Georgia muttered.

"Then I took her to lunch."

"A Happy Meal at McDonald's?" Georgia asked, hoping the sarcastic reference would remind him of just how young Emily was.

Spencer laughed. "Come on, Georgia, I would never take a woman to lunch at a fast food joint. I took her to that new little pasta place on Oakland."

Georgia's vision went red. This was no *woman*— this was her daughter! The choice of restaurant sent her suspicions soaring. The process had started: long, intimate lunches in trendy little places.

This couldn't be happening. Couldn't Emily see the man was too old for her?

Georgia watched him as he shuffled through the sheaf of messages she'd placed on his worktable. His hair was even more mussed than usual, blown by the sultry May breezes to fall just right over his forehead. His shirtsleeves were rolled to reveal tanned, leanly muscled arms. His profile was firm, intriguing. Who was she kidding? Spencer Foxworth wasn't too old for anyone.

Spencer was surprised to look up and find Georgia staring at him. He put down the stack of messages, moving across the room toward her.

"What's the matter, sweetheart? You look all flustered about something." And indeed she did. She also looked very pretty in a heated sort of way. "You look hot."

She felt hot. Why was he standing so close?

"I was thinking about taking a swim. Why don't you join me? I'm sure there's a bathing suit around here somewhere that would fit you." The invitation had come off the top of his head, but the idea was really starting to appeal to him. Georgia in a bathing suit...

"I probably have a few steaks in the freezer. Stay for supper." Georgia on the beach in the moonlight, reflections from a bonfire playing in her honey-colored hair...

"No thanks. I don't intend to wear any hand-me-downs left by a member of your harem."

Spencer grinned. "No problem. I don't mind swimming in the nude if you don't."

Georgia glared at him, all the while trying not to see him as he'd looked that long-ago morning, naked in the sunlight. "I hear freshwater sharks can be just as dangerous as the kind you find in the ocean." She picked up her purse and started for the door. "I think I'll pass."

"Coward," his voice teased from behind her.

She turned around. The challenge in his eyes almost got to her. Almost—until she remembered who he'd been with all afternoon. How dare he spend the day with her daughter, then turn around and propose a moonlight swim with her? "Not afraid, Spencer, just sensible. Sharks bite."

Spencer watched the door slam behind her, and he chuckled to himself. He thought he'd had her there for a minute. His next thought immediately sobered him. She'd almost had him for a moment, as well. What was he thinking of—a moonlight swim with the uptight Ms. Moon? Hell, what he'd been thinking of was the possible lushness of her statuesque figure under all those clothes. What he'd been thinking of was the look of her lying in the waves in the moonlight.

Heat infused his body and he turned away from the door, running a hand through his hair, going out on the patio for a little air. The lake breeze brought relief from the heat of the afternoon, cooled him down. Which was exactly what he needed. Hot thoughts about Ms. Georgia Moon would get him nowhere. Someone young and carefree like Emily was who he should be thinking about. So why wasn't he?

LEANING ON THE SCREEN door, quart container of ice cream in her hand, Georgia stared out into the darkened yard. It was getting time to plant flowers. Usually by now she'd be planning the color scheme, browsing at the nursery.

Every year the borders were perfect, the grass smooth, the yard well groomed. Every year she painted the porch floor, washed the windows inside and out, sent the curtains to the cleaners, got the carpet shampooed. All it took was living right. That's what Georgia had always believed.

If you baked cookies for the PTA, your child would go to college. If you became a Brownie leader, your child would never cheat or steal. If you never missed a school play, a Christmas concert or a birthday party, everything was supposed to turn out like it should.

So why hadn't it?

"Chocolate marshmallow—that's always been your favorite poison."

Georgia sighed, her body slumping slightly against the screen. "Please, Mother, don't lecture me about fats and emulsifiers now. I'm in no mood for it."

"I wouldn't dream of it, love. You must be very troubled."

"What makes you say that?"

"Chocolate marshmallow has always been your refuge in times of trouble."

Georgia smiled wearily. "Yeah, but you used to make me put wheat germ on it."

Jasmine came close, reaching up to run her hand up and down Georgia's back, leaning her head on her daughter's shoulder. "I know it was hard for you, the way I was. I know that all you wanted was a mother who wore polyester pantsuits and who baked brownies for the PTA."

"Well, maybe not polyester—"

Jasmine laughed softly. "My point is, I couldn't be what you wanted, I had to be myself, just as Emily has to be herself now."

Georgia shoved the spoon into the half-empty carton. "But what about me? *I'm* just being *myself!*"

"Are you?"

Georgia frowned. "What does that mean?"

"You can't continue to live vicariously through your daughter, Georgia. It's not good for a child to have a mother who's denied herself so much of life."

Georgia turned on her. "Oh? And what do you think *is* good for a child? A mother so wrapped up in her art that she can't even take the time to come to a school play? A father you can't keep track of because he moves his canvas and easel to a different country every other month? Should a child have to plan asking her mother a question, or needing her mother's love, by the amount of light coming in the studio?"

"You always had my love," Jasmine said softly.

The fight went out of Georgia. "Oh, Mother, I know. And I've always loved you, too. It's just that—"

"It's just that you wanted to give your daughter a different kind of life," Jasmine finished for her. "I understand, really I do, but did you ever think that maybe lace curtains aren't the answer? When you married so young I knew you were looking for stability, looking for roots I couldn't provide, but—"

Georgia snorted. "Lot of good it did me."

"Just because a man wears a suit to work, doesn't mean he's good husband and father material, Georgia."

"You can say that again. Emily hears from her father even less than I hear from mine. Funny, isn't it? I tried so hard to make sure it would be different, but I ended up raising my child alone, just like you did."

"You've done a good job with her, Georgia, just as I have with you. Now it's time to let go. You can't deny your daughter a chance at happiness by some misguided idea of how she should live her life."

"Oh, and you think intimate lunches with Spencer Foxworth offer her a chance for happiness?" Georgia bit out.

A glint of amusement lightened Jasmine's eyes. "Well, now we're getting down to it, aren't we? That's what has you going tonight, isn't it? It's no longer just Emily dropping out of college. It's the idea of them together that has you so riled."

"Well, wouldn't it rile you?" Georgia looked her mother up and down. "No, I guess it wouldn't, would it?"

"Only if I wanted him for myself."

"That's ridiculous!"

"Is it?"

"Of course—"

"Well, maybe so. But it's something you should think about. The right woman could keep him so busy he wouldn't have time to even *think* of getting his hands on your daughter."

Chapter Three

Spencer bent over his worktable, exhibiting the intense concentration that always surprised Georgia. The blazing sun flashed off the Rolex strapped to one brown, sinewy arm as he lifted a hand to brush his rumpled hair—a gesture she had seen him make a thousand times. So why did the sight of that masculine limb disturb her so today?

Why, indeed. Jasmine's words of the night before floated just outside her ear, like a ghost intent on haunting. *Only if I wanted him for myself....*

Absurd. Of course Georgia didn't want him for herself. Why, she could have had him for herself years ago if she'd wanted him. For a while, anyway. That was all any woman ever got Spencer Foxworth for—a while. And that was what was bothering her. He would break Emily's heart and she would have to stand by and watch it happen. Because Emily wouldn't listen if Georgia tried to warn her. Daughters never did listen to their mothers about these things. Georgia certainly hadn't listened to Jasmine when she'd made up her mind to marry so young.

And what else had Jasmine said last night while Georgia stuffed herself with ice cream? Something about the right woman making Spencer forget all about seducing Emily. But Georgia could never be that woman. Could she?

Spencer threw down his pencil and stretched, reaching his leanly muscled arms ceilingward and then back to clasp together behind his head. "Well, Georgia," he said over his shoulder, "that's one more thing crossed off that infinite list of yours."

"Hmm?" she answered lazily.

Spence swiveled his head in her direction, one brow raised. She sounded uncharacteristically tired. He peered at her through the fretwork of shelves that separated his work area from Georgia's, but her face was in shadow. "You will be happy to know that I just finished the parti for the Hawkins house. You can give Eloise a call and set up a meeting."

"That's nice," Georgia murmured.

Spencer's brows came down in a frown. "Georgia, are you listening to me?"

"Hmm?"

Spencer slid off his stool, walking around the partition till he stood in front of Georgia's desk. She sat with her head propped in her hand, her eyes out of focus, a small frown on her forehead. She didn't seem aware that he was there.

"Georgia?" He leaned forward to read the paper under her hand. Oh, yes, his bank statement. He'd been meaning to talk to her about what a mess it was in this month. He was always forgetting to enter check amounts in the register or record advances from ATMs. Somehow she always managed to untangle the labyrinth he left his finances in. Right next to the jumbled statement was a bill of lading for a special-order light-fixture shipment that had somehow never reached its destination. If he knew Georgia, she'd have it tracked down and rerouted to its proper destination by nightfall.

What would he do without her? She steadied his life, kept it all together, made it possible for him to keep his devil-may-care attitude toward work. He was well aware of all that she brought to his life. For the first time, he wondered just what he brought to hers. Why did she put up with him? She was smart enough, good enough at her job to have moved on years ago. Now that he thought of it, he wondered why she hadn't. Now that he thought of it, he was extremely *glad* she hadn't.

He reached over, tapping a finger on the paper under her hand. "See you got the bank statement, huh?"

Georgia shook herself out of her pondering. "Hmm?" She looked down. "Oh—yeah."

"Well, aren't you going to say anything?" He figured he was in for the usual lecture on financial responsibility. In fact, he'd come to look forward to their verbal sparring.

Now, instead of the stimulating little debate he'd counted on, Georgia merely looked up at him and said, "I'll get it straightened out."

Her big hazel eyes, flecked with amber, glowed softly. Her thick honey-colored hair curved against her jawline, wispy bangs brushing her brows. Her mouth was small, full, a little pouty. Kissable. Staring at it, he could remember how it felt when he'd touched it briefly all those years ago—warm, soft, pliant—

Spencer blinked and looked away. Where on earth were these thoughts coming from? Last night, moonlit swims; today, morning kisses. Something definitely was different in how he was thinking of Ms. Georgia Moon.

He looked at her again. Her eyes were still on him, dreamy, a little wistful. Was she seeing something different, too?

Georgia was caught in that navy-blue gaze. Then the ghost repeated, *Only if I wanted him for myself...* and she jumped, almost as if she could feel cool breath at her ear. Her eyes focused on the papers under her hand.

"You know, Spencer," she said, back to her usual briskness, "this mess wouldn't be nearly as daunting if I had a nice fat check from your last project to deposit.''

Spencer laughed. ''Georgia, Georgia—you had me worried there for a minute.'' Hell, he'd had himself worried. Her tone was reassuring; this was Ms. Moon, his prim, proper assistant. ''For a minute there, I thought we were actually going to get through the day without one of our little debates.''

''Well, you should be worried. That project cost you—''

''We're not going to get into that again, are we? You know profit is not the bottom line for me. That couple—''

''You mean that girl, don't you? She worked her wiles on you and you fell for it.''

''Come on, Georgia, give me a little more credit than that. They were young and in love. They ran into trouble, and when they couldn't pay my fee—''

''You waived it,'' Georgia finished for him in exasperation. ''Honestly, Spencer, you have no business sense at all. You turn down half the projects you're offered, for the most ridiculous reasons—''

''Refusing to compromise my creative integrity is not a ridiculous reason.''

''Then when you *do* work, you cut your fees, or even waive them, at the drop of a hat—''

Spencer held up a finger. ''I did that once.''

''And isn't once enough?''

Spence shrugged, shoving his hands into his loose cotton pants. "Look, they were a sweet couple. They ran into some problems and I wanted to help."

Georgia made a little derisive sound in her throat, and Spencer took his hands out of his pockets, placed them flat on the desk and leaned forward. He looked into those skeptical hazel eyes. "You got something against love, George?" His mouth twisted into a grin, fanning tiny crinkles out around eyes that were bluer than the May sky.

Georgia wondered why lines always looked better on a man's face than on a woman's. Her gaze wandered down to his mouth. His top lip was sculptured; his lower lip fuller, softer. Her eyes met his again. He seemed to be waiting for an answer. She swallowed. "What was the question?"

"I said," he began softly, so softly that her gaze shifted to those lips again, watching them form the words, "have you got something against love, George?"

For the first time, she became aware that he was calling her George, the hated nickname her mother always used. It sounded different on his tongue—intimate, playful, sexy. A sense of danger seemed to crackle in the heated air and he was suddenly closer—closer than before. Georgia's eyes moved back up to his, but the question there was gone, replaced by something deeper, something she couldn't grasp—something she didn't want to grasp. Before she could pull away, before she could break that dangerous heat between them, he touched his mouth to hers in a kiss that was soft, tantalizing, barely there.

When it was over, he just stared at her, looking as surprised as she felt, looking like—looking like he wanted to do it again.

She stood up abruptly, gathering papers, tapping them against the desk to form a neat pile. "No," she said, her voice brisk again, the husky laziness gone, "I don't have anything against love. I just don't believe in it. And don't call me George!"

SPENCER WAS SHAKEN. He'd kissed her. One sign of encouragement from her and he'd still be kissing her—and doing a lot more if she'd let him. Instead he was barreling down the highway, pushing the Jag past the speed limit, heading for the site. He didn't need to be there today—Vinnie had things well under control, and normally he wouldn't be checking it out again until the next week. But he had to get out of there, away from Georgia. He had to think, and he didn't know where else to go.

He found Vinnie leaning on the back of his old panel truck, squinting at a print. "You here again?" Vinnie asked.

"Yeah," Spencer grumbled, "but don't ask me why."

Vinnie looked up from the print, narrowing his eyes on Spencer's face. "Got troubles?"

Spence leaned against the dusty truck, crossing his arms. "Vin, have you ever known a woman for a long time, and then all of a sudden—"

Vinnie grinned. "Georgia Moon has finally risen."

"What's that supposed to mean?"

"Hell, Foxworth, it's like a summer storm. Takes a long time comin' but you can see it for miles."

Spencer didn't say anything for a moment. There was a hesitant, almost nervous, quality to his voice when he finally asked, "So—what do you think?"

"About Ms. Moon and you? I'd say it was inevitable—and about time."

Spencer shook his head. "Think you know it all, don't you?"

Vinnie shrugged. "I know a good match when I see one."

"What are you talking about? We're exact opposites. Oil and water."

Vinnie squinted into the sun, thinking about it. "Naw. With Ms. Moon I'd say it was closer to oil and vinegar. Just remember, the combination makes one hell of a salad dressing. You just got to add a few spices and shake it up once in a while."

"That's quite an analogy. Is that how you thought of your relationship with Carol? Dressing on the salad bar of life?"

Vinnie shook his head, staring at the dusty ground. "Carol and I had our signals crossed. I thought I was buying all-you-can-eat—she had one-trip-only in mind."

"Three years is a little more than one trip, Vin. It's a long time to spend on one woman."

Vinnie looked at him. "Not if it's the right woman."

"You still think Carol was the right woman?"

Vinnie shook his head. "Nope." He grinned suddenly. "Anyway, good buddy, we weren't talking about Carol. We were talking about Georgia Moon."

"The lady's got *wrong woman* written all over her—wrong for me, anyway. Georgia is rules and conventions, home and hearth. Everything I've always avoided."

"Yeah? Then what's the problem?"

Spencer didn't answer. He just walked to his car, slid in and drove away.

What *was* the problem? he asked himself as he aimlessly followed the shore of Lake Michigan.

The problem was, Georgia was not the kind of woman a man could satisfy his curiosity about, then casually move on. She was a keeper.

And that should be scaring the hell out of him. Shouldn't it?

Was Vinnie right? Had it been a long time coming? He searched his memory. Ten years was a long

time, but he remembered the day he'd met Georgia
like it was yesterday.

She had come to him in answer to an ad he'd
placed in an alternative east-side newspaper. He
needed an assistant—someone to run interference
with clients, someone to answer the phone, someone to keep track of his finances. At thirty, Spencer
Foxworth had even less interest in the mundane
tasks of everyday living than he did today. But he
hadn't wanted the usual secretary who would quib-
ble over job descriptions, balk at picking up his
laundry or doing a little shopping. So he'd turned to
the little weekly, knowing its readership was as out
of the mainstream as its news.

Okay, he'd admit it. He'd had visions of some
long-legged, flaxen-haired, former flower child
coming to him with her bare feet and warm heart.
What he'd gotten was Georgia Moon, an attractive,
feisty young divorcee with a hands-off look in her
eyes, and a nine-year-old daughter waiting in her
battered station wagon.

He still remembered his one and only glimpse of
Emily, a wide-eyed skinny little kid, staring at him
through a dusty car window. When he'd smiled at
her, she'd stuck out her tongue and thumbed her
nose at him.

Georgia proved to have almost no experience and
a certificate from a nine-month accounting course.
Spence had envisioned her spending the last of her

divorce settlement on it. He'd also envisioned that snotty little kid going to bed without supper. So he abandoned the daydream of the long-haired nymph and hired Georgia Moon.

She'd hated his house, hated his life, maybe even hated him. But he'd never been sorry.

Spencer looked at the lengthening shadows and lowering sun, deciding to make a U-turn and head back home, thinking that what he'd felt that morning when he'd looked into those clear hazel eyes, smelled the warmth of that pale skin, and kissed the soft surprise of that mouth, was a long way from just never being sorry.

ONLY IF I WANTED him for myself.... The ghost was in the car, sitting right beside her, whispering in her ear again. *Only if I wanted him for myself....*

Georgia switched on the radio, turning the volume up to drown out the whisper. But of course it was a love song. And of course it made her think of dancing, the cheek-to-cheek, chest-to-chest kind. Swaying beneath the stars or in a darkened nightclub, the other people mere shadows in the candlelight—

Absurd. She had never known that kind of love. The kind that walked in the moonlight, the kind that held hands to the late show. Georgia switched off the radio.

Her husband had not been a man who danced under the stars or anywhere else. And, to be honest, that had been one of the reasons she'd married him. He'd seemed so solid, so stable, so reliable compared to her crazy artist parents. Unfortunately, all those hours he'd put in at the office weren't spent working. One call from his secretary informing her of what was going on was all it took for her to march out the door and take back her maiden name. The really hard part had been admitting that her parents, in their own crazy way, had more fidelity in their unconventional union than her buttoned-down husband had given her in their holy marriage.

Georgia pulled the car up in front of her house and cut the engine. She sat looking at the house, thinking about the long night ahead with not much else to do but needlepoint another pillow.

What was wrong with her lately? Why think about the past, about her husband, after all this time?

But she knew the answer. As much as she didn't want to admit it, ever since last night, ever since her mother had put the notion into her head, she'd been wondering what it would be like to be with a whole other kind of man. A man who was spontaneous, a man who knew how to live, a man who was a little wild—a man like Spencer Foxworth.

WHEN SPENCER WALKED IN the door, the phone was ringing.

"Spencer Foxworth," he answered crisply.

"The great man answers his own phone."

It took him only a moment to recognize the voice. "Emily?"

"Right the first time. I'm flattered—not only that you answered the phone yourself, but that you recognized my voice."

Spencer smiled into the receiver. "Don't be too flattered. Your mother left almost two hours ago."

"Really? Hmm—she's not home yet."

Spencer felt a tug of absurd worry at that; after all, what did he really know of Georgia's life? She could have met a woman friend for an early dinner, or she could have a date with a man—or she could be lying, hurt and anonymous, in a hospital somewhere. Apparently, Emily felt no such concern.

"The reason I'm calling, a friend of mine is having his first show—functional sculpture. The opening's tomorrow night. I thought it might interest you."

Spencer forced his mind off Georgia—and who she might be with—and onto the young, vital voice in his ear. "Are you asking me for a date?"

"Right again. For an old guy, you're pretty quick on the draw. How about it?"

Yes, thought Spencer, how about it? Might be just the thing to get him back on track. "Sounds great. Do I pick you up or are you too liberated for that?''

Emily laughed. ''And miss riding in that Jag? Not a chance. See you around seven?''

''Seven it is.''

DRIVING THROUGH the early evening toward his ''date'' with Emily Moon, Spencer found himself in a pleasant state of anticipation. There hadn't been a woman in his life for quite a while. He found himself wondering if George was the reason. He'd been acting pretty crazy lately—finding an excuse to see where she lived, talking about her to Vinnie. And then yesterday—he had kissed her—teasingly, of course. But for just those few moments, something had passed between them and he had wanted her. Today, though, it was as if the moment had never happened. She was her old self, brisk and efficient.

He'd told himself he was relieved. He told himself that taking Emily out would once and for all end the crazy thoughts he'd been thinking lately. Georgia Moon wasn't for him. Too many rules, too many walls. He'd been raised by a grandmother, the matriarch in a family of old money. By the time he'd struck out on his own, he'd had enough rules and obligations to last him a lifetime. He lived in a house without walls, a world without boundaries. He intended to keep it that way.

He pulled up in front of the tiny Cape Cod, jumped out of the Jag and strolled up the walk. It was pleasantly warm, and a soft breeze stirred the old-fashioned rosebushes flanking the stairs, sending their fragrance into the night. He bent and plucked one for an offering. Soft music came through the screen door. He smiled when he recognized the tune. Johnny Mathis—"Chances Are." He stood listening for a minute, then rang the doorbell.

Peering through the screen, he expected to see Emily bouncing down the stairs toward him. But it was Georgia—Georgia in a long white robe—and his heart almost stopped.

She was modestly tightening the belt at her waist, but nothing could cover up the glimpse of long, shapely leg showing through the opening of the wrap robe as she descended. His gaze moved down to her feet, long and narrow, well shaped—and bare. The surprise on her face at the sight of him matched his own, and for a moment they just stood and stared at each other.

Spence swallowed. "Hi," he managed to get out.

Georgia clutched the lapels of her robe and pulled them together, holding them close to her throat, but not before he saw the gleam of pearly skin, the whisper of cleavage.

"I—I wasn't expecting you."

"Weren't you?" he asked, unable to take his eyes off her. Her skin was dewy and slightly flushed. Her hair was damp, little wavy tendrils clinging to her forehead and cheeks. She looked— She looked touchable. Spencer had the uncomfortable feeling that if the screen hadn't been between them he'd be doing just that—touching her.

Georgia cleared her throat. "Do you want something?"

He let out a long breath, a grin spreading over his face. "Oh, George, that's not a question to ask a man when you're standing there dressed like that."

Georgia clutched tighter at the robe. "I just got out of the shower and since I wasn't expecting anyone, least of all you—" She stopped and frowned. "What are you doing here, anyway?"

"Mom," Emily said from behind her, "aren't you going to invite my date in? We're going to a gallery opening."

Georgia whipped around to see Emily coming down the stairs. Emily in short, tight white, her tanned arms bare, the glint of long, gold earrings at her ears. Emily—a woman.

She whipped back around to gape at Spencer. And he was certainly a man, standing there in a crisp linen suit, shirt open at the throat, hands clutching a rose.

Oh, God, a rose! And from *her* own bushes! Georgia felt faint. Maybe she should do just that—

faint dead at their feet. They'd have to forget this ridiculous date and rush her to the hospital— *wouldn't they?* She got a mental flash of Spencer stepping right over her prone body and waltzing out the door, her daughter on his arm, without a backward glance.

"I'll just get my purse, Spencer, then I'll be right with you," Emily said. Georgia turned to see her running lightly up the stairs, then turned back to Spencer.

But Spencer wasn't watching Emily, he was still staring at Georgia. *Don't do this,* she wanted to say, but the words caught in her throat.

Why was she looking at him like he was the big bad wolf out to eat her baby lamb? She looked so darn worried, so damn vulnerable. And that soft, white robe—he could feel his fingers itching to reach out and loosen the tie that held it together. Reach into its folds... Touch—

"All set," Emily said brightly from the staircase.

Spencer tore his gaze off Georgia and onto his date, where it belonged. What the hell was the matter with him? How could he be going out with one woman while wanting another?

Emily breezed past him and out the door. "Are you coming?" she called.

He looked again at Georgia. "Look, Georgia, I—"

"Get her home safe and sound and at a decent hour—or—or—"

Spencer's mouth hardened. "Or what, George?"

"Or—or you'll be sorry," Georgia finished lamely. "And don't call me George!"

She stood in the doorway and watched him walk down the steps toward her daughter. His chestnut hair ruffled in the evening breeze, his linen suit draped his body beautifully. She hated to admit it, but he looked fantastic—maybe better than she'd ever seen him look. She watched him open the car door for Emily, hand her the rose, then circle the Jag and climb in beside her. The perfect escort. The perfect gentleman. Except this was no gentleman— this was Spencer Foxworth!

"I'm going to kill him," she said aloud.

"That might be a little drastic, love," Jasmine said from behind her. "Might I make another suggestion?"

Georgia turned around. "Please do."

"Go after him."

"What?"

"Go upstairs, put on something alluring and go after him."

"What? He's going to take a look at me in my one and only cocktail dress and suddenly forget that he's out with a beautiful twenty-year-old? Mother, the man has been looking at me for ten long years. It's going to take more than a little black silk to get him interested.''

"Maybe not," Jasmine murmured.

Georgia looked at her sharply. "What did you say?''

"Nothing," Jasmine replied innocently. "You know, even if you couldn't get his mind off Emily, you could at least find out what was going on between the two of them.''

"Mother, are you suggesting I spy on my own daughter?''

Jasmine sighed. "You're right, love, it's too outrageous for *you* to even contemplate.''

Outrageous. Georgia turned the word over in her mind. Outrageous times called for outrageous measures. She started for the stairs.

"Where are you going, love?''

"I'm going to shake the wrinkles out of my black silk ... and then I'm going after them.''

"You mean you're going to the gallery opening?''

Georgia stopped halfway up the stairs. "It's open to the public, isn't it?''

"Of course.''

"Well, that's me—the public. Spencer Fox-worth's public enemy number one!''

Chapter Four

Despite the beautiful young Emily on his arm, Spencer was feeling his age. His casual linen suit was a trifle too elegant amid the jeans, miniskirts and bermuda shorts of the twenty-something crowd.

Emily took his hand. "There's Gregor. Come meet him."

Gregor looked more like a brat-packer whose trust-fund allowance had run out than an artist. True, his madras bermudas were frayed around the hems and fashionably ripped, but the white T-shirt had the kind of cut that let you know right away that it cost ten times what Vinnie probably paid for his. His blond hair was long and expensively cut, and the hand he held out to Spencer felt like it had never known a day's labor.

"Cool," the young man stated upon hearing Spencer's name. "I love your houses, man."

Spencer winced. "Thanks. Congratulations on your first showing."

"Yeah," the young man replied offhandedly, gesturing arrogantly toward the nearly empty room. "Take a look around, Foxworth. If you see something you like maybe we can cut a deal."

Spencer winced again and Emily wisely led him off. "Cut a deal?" he said when they were out of earshot. "This guy doing a little sculpting between semesters at business school?"

Emily laughed. "His dad's some big-shot corporate monster and Gregor hasn't quite gotten it out of his system yet."

"I bet you called him Greg in high school, and he was captain of the golf team."

Emily gave him a teasing smile. "Something like that." She took his arm. "Now, don't be a snob, Spencer. Give the guy a chance—you haven't even looked at his stuff yet."

His "stuff" turned out to be a lot of lengths of copper piping and slabs of granite made into benches, tables and stiff-looking chairs. One particularly offensive piece was the semblance of a grandfather clock, with hands shaped like bird's wings fastened to its pink granite face. A small white card read *Time Flies*. Spencer stifled a laugh.

After a while, Emily asked, "Well, what do you think?"

"Very organic," Spencer answered with mock seriousness. "The use of recycled pipe, with its soft green patina, makes one want to coin the phrase *ecologically correct functional sculpture.*"

Emily poked him in the ribs with an elbow. "Okay, okay—it's pretty horrible, I agree." Her gaze fixed on Gregor, who was glad-handing people over near the table that held the cheap champagne and runny Brie, and she made a face. "And so is Gregor—I mean Greg," she conceded. "Seeing him again makes me remember how irritating I always found him."

"You don't know how relieved I am to hear it," replied Spencer dryly.

"I'll take that as a compliment." She took his hand again. "Come with me. There's something I want to show you."

She led him over to a door and opened it. The small room beyond was dark until Emily flipped a switch and pale blue light illuminated the form that rose nearly to the ceiling. It leapt to life, one vast, flowing surface, unmarred by detail but intimating a feminine form, reaching for the sky. Slowly it turned on its base, the light on the lustrous surface suggesting movement, graceful and supple. And then it was gone, its edge barely visible, until it turned, dancing into the light once again.

"It's beautiful," Spencer whispered, knowing the term to be trite, inadequate. He turned to the girl at his side. "It's yours, isn't it?"

Emily nodded. "I call it *Moondancer.*"

Spencer walked around the sculpture. It had power, grace; it made him react, made him think. If the piece could do all that in this small, jumbled workroom Emily was hiding it in, what could it do once released to a space worthy of it? This girl had talent. Surely Georgia could see that? "What does your mother think of it?"

Emily shrugged. "Mom hasn't seen it."

"But why? Surely if you showed her—"

"It wouldn't do any good."

"That I can't believe."

"Huh, you don't know Mom. She's a real stickler for a college education."

Spencer's eyes followed the piece. It was big and bold, yet utterly feminine. Like Georgia herself—steel and curves, strength and illusion. "What if you sold it?" he asked.

"Yeah, that might make a difference with her. Even if it didn't, I'd have the money to strike out on my own, to start a new piece." She shrugged negligently. "That's not very likely, though. Who'd buy it? It hasn't even been shown."

"I'll buy it."

Emily stared at him. "What?"

"I said, I'll buy it. Name your price."

Emily continued to stare at him for a moment, and then a smile started to spread across her face. "You're serious, aren't you?"

Spencer nodded. "Dead serious. You, Emily Moon, are going to be a name one day. You've got talent."

"Well, I know, but—"

"I want *Moondancer,* Emily. What's it going to cost me?"

GEORGIA'S GAZE MOVED furiously around the gallery, but she couldn't spot them anywhere. Damn, she was probably too late. She shouldn't have let Jasmine talk her into that quick hem job on her dress. True, the shorter length brought her black silk sheath into the nineties, but the job had taken too long, and now it looked like her mission had failed before it even had a chance to begin. Obviously, Spencer and Emily had already left.

She wobbled on heels that were a little too high, in shoes she could barely remember buying that Jasmine had unearthed from the bottom of her closet. Carefully she made her way over to the refreshment table. She was hot in her panty hose and silk, and thought maybe just a little glass of cool white wine ...

She was standing and sipping when she noticed a door opening at the far end of the gallery, a very familiar chestnut head appearing from behind it. And there was Emily, looking up at him like he was some knight in shining armor—except he was Spencer Foxworth in baggy linen, and the only thing shining about him was the lurid look in his navy-blue eyes.

The man couldn't even wait to get her somewhere private before he made his move, but had dragged poor Emily into a closet for a private little grope session.

Georgia tossed back the rest of her wine, slammed the glass on the table and picked up a full one. Sidling over toward a giant column of granite with several arms of copper sticking out at all angles, she pretended to study it from behind, her eyes constantly darting to the far end of the room.

Spencer looked over Emily's shoulder and did a double take. My God, was that Georgia peering out from behind pink granite? Impossible. The woman had been so much on his mind lately, he was starting to hallucinate. He turned back to Emily, trying to focus on what she was saying. But his eyes kept wandering over to the other end of the room.

Whoever was hiding behind that sculpture had the same honey-blond hair, red-gold hidden in the waves, darker, richer than Emily's icy white locks. The head peeked around one of the arms and Spencer got a good look at the woman's mouth before she disappeared again. Emily's mouth was wide, generous, bright with moist color. This woman's was smaller, a little pouty, softly naked—just like Georgia's.

A couple wandered over to study the sculpture and the woman had to shift a little to make room for them. Spencer caught a glimpse of a long, shapely leg in dark stockings and high, high heels. His mind flashed back to the sight of Georgia descending the stairs earlier, the flash of shapely leg through her robe. His eyes narrowed.

"Spencer, are you listening to me?"

"I think that's your mother over there, hiding behind that sculpture."

"What?" Emily swung around just as the woman disappeared again. "Impossible. My mother never wears her skirts that short. Besides, what would she be doing—" Emily took another look. "Oh, no— she's spying on us! Of all the—"

Emily took off across the room. "Mother, come out from behind there."

"Why, Emily, what are you doing here?"

"Come off it, Mother. You know what *I'm* doing here. The question is, what are *you* doing here?"

"Well, you're always complaining that I don't take any interest in art. So I thought—"

"Right." Emily rolled her eyes before placing her hands on her hips, looking like a smaller but just as stern version of Georgia on the warpath. "Will you stop interfering in my life? Showing up here and spying on me isn't going to get me to go back to school. I'm going to the ladies' room, Mother. I hope you'll have the good grace to be gone by the time I get back."

Georgia watched Emily march off, wondering if she should follow her. Wondering if she should take a stab at warning her off Spencer Foxworth. If Spencer had already tried to ravish her with about fifty people around, what would he do when he got her into that sleek, too sexy car on a dark street somewhere? Or back at his place after a walk on the beach, snuggling up to a fire in that hideous circular fireplace. Or—

"My, my, my—fancy meeting you here."

Georgia spun around and almost fell from her high heels into Spencer Foxworth's arms. "Spencer!"

"In the flesh."

"What a surprise."

"For me, maybe. For you, I don't think so."

She tried backing away from him, but he moved right along with her. Her back hit the wall, and there was nowhere else to go. Instead of cooling her off, the two glasses of wine she'd downed seemed to be heating her up. Or was it just because he was standing so close? He raised his arm, bracing a hand on the wall near her head. She started to sidle away, but he brought his other arm up, trapping her.

He could smell her light, fresh perfume and the sweetness of her breath as it came a little hard between her parted lips. She looked confused—appealingly so. He leaned in closer.

"Were you looking for me?" he murmured.

"Of course not. Why would I be looking for you?"

He leaned back a little, moving his gaze over her. "I don't know. You show up looking like a woman who's trying to make an impression—maybe you're a little jealous."

"Jealous? Don't be ridiculous!" stammered Georgia. The arrogance of the man.

"Then what are you doing here?"

"I know your reputation, Spencer. For ten long years I've watched you love 'em and leave 'em. Maybe I'm just trying to see that that doesn't happen to Emily."

His eyes narrowed. "Spying, were you? What do you take me for? Do you really think I'd do anything to hurt your daughter?"

"I think you'd do anything to get what you want. You always have—you always will."

His eyes moved over her face. His voice came softly, languidly. "And what if it isn't Emily I want?"

Georgia swallowed. "Then what is it you *do* want?" she whispered with a dry mouth.

He leaned closer, his gaze riveted to her mouth. Soft, sweet. Then he looked into her eyes—those amber sparks amid the hazel . . . just a little hungry, just a little searching. An arrow of need shot through him. He could slake that hunger, end that search, drink from that mouth, feed his own need. All he had to do was move a little closer—

Emily came up alongside of him, jerking his arm away from the wall. "If you won't leave, Mother, then we will. Come on, Spencer."

She pulled him away and he went, shaken, confused, still full of need. At the door, he looked over his shoulder. Georgia was still standing there, looking like the mama sheep witnessing the wolf leading her lamb to slaughter. What did she think he was?

Let her stew, he thought. Grinning at her, he gave her a little salute and turned back to Emily.

GEORGIA TOSSED and turned, constantly looking at the alarm clock on her bedside table. Where were they—and what were they doing? And what was the matter with Emily? Georgia had raised her to have more sense than to fall for a man who would flirt with—and worse, almost kiss—another woman while he was on a date. The fact that that other woman was her own mother should have given the situation even more weight. Shouldn't it?

Or maybe not. Maybe Emily figured old, staid, boring Mom was no competition at all. Georgia beat at her pillow, trying to whip it into some magical shape that would let her sleep, angry at the thought, even though she knew it was probably true.

And what kind of game was Spencer playing, anyway? He had been so close. She could have sworn his lips were moving in for the kill. She groaned and buried her face in her beaten pillow. The heat rose over her, the same heat she'd felt watching that mouth loom closer. She couldn't blame it on the wine this time. So she'd blame it on the anger. Somehow she'd think of a way to get Emily out of his clutches—if she had to lie awake all night to do it!

GEORGIA STORMED into work on Monday morning loaded for fire. She'd spent a lousy weekend, worrying and fretting. For two days, Emily had industriously and creatively, with the help of Jasmine, managed to avoid her. Georgia had been left to work out her frustration cleaning closets, a chore she loathed under the best of circumstances. Now she was ready to take out those frustrations on Spencer Foxworth.

But instead of finding Spencer waiting for her in the crescent-shaped house without walls, she found a cloud of smoke, behind which sat Eloise Hawkins in all her tanned, hair-sprayed and gold-chained glory.

"Well, it's about time somebody got here. Just where is that cute boss of yours hiding this morning?"

"I don't know...." Georgia looked up toward the loft.

"Forget it, honey. I already checked the bedroom. That's the first place I'd expect to find a man like Spencer Foxworth. But—" she laughed and coughed, spewing smoke toward Georgia "—no such luck. And I had the cutest little way in mind of waking him up."

"I'll just bet," Georgia murmured. More directly, she said, "I'm sure he'll be here any minute, Mrs. Hawkins. He wouldn't want to keep you waiting for long."

"Honey, a woman could wait forever with a man like— Why, speak of the devil. And I *do* mean devil—"

Georgia looked to find Spencer crossing the patio, dripping water, a blue towel slung low around his waist.

"Eloise, I'm sorry. Have you been waiting long? Guess I lost track of the time."

"Sugar, the wait was well worth it," Eloise drawled.

Georgia could practically make out the drool on Eloise Hawkins's chin. Disgusting, even though Georgia had to admit there was plenty there to drool over. The lightly tanned, nicely defined muscles, the rivulets of water chasing each other down slick, wet chest hair, disappearing beneath the towel, drawing attention to what was underneath it. Those intensely blue, laughing eyes. That mouth that—

Georgia was feeling warm again, in a way that had little to do with the unseasonable heat wave.

Spencer strode toward the loft. "I'll just be a minute, Eloise. Make yourself at home."

"Honey, if I do that I'm liable to shock Ms. Moon here to death."

Spencer chuckled and turned around. Although his eyes sought Eloise, his gaze ran right past her to Georgia. The prim Ms. Moon. No short skirt this time, no spike heels, no hungry look in her eyes. Had he imagined the look? Had he imagined the air crackling and sizzling between them? Or was Ms. Georgia Moon just one very good actress? Maybe if Eloise Hawkins wasn't waiting, he'd have shed his towel and found out.

ELOISE HAWKINS KNEW exactly what she wanted, and what she wanted was a whirlpool in the master bath and a hot tub just off the back deck. Arthur would not be pleased. Georgia sat taking notes, playing the good little assistant. Maybe it was just as well she hadn't had a chance to have it out with Spencer. The direct approach probably wouldn't work with him. She needed something more devious—something more Spencer Foxworthlike.

"Eloise," Spencer was saying, "you must remember the meeting where you and Arthur and I sat down and worked out a budget—"

"Spencer, honey, you're a man of considerable charm. I have faith that you'll be able to get old Arthur to dig a little bit deeper into his pockets." Eloise leaned forward, displaying unnaturally dark, bony cleavage. "I want that hot tub."

Spencer ignored the woman's offering and let his voice go a shade deeper. "And you, my lovely Eloise, being an attractive, persuasive woman, are surely the best candidate to demonstrate just what that hot tub could mean to your marriage."

Eloise raised her well-tended hand to pat her hair, the charm bracelet on her skinny wrist jangling in confusion. The slash of pink mouth smirked against the tanning booth bronze of her skin. She attempted a throaty laugh but all she got was a hacking cough, reminding her to light another long, narrow, flower-bedecked cigarette.

"Now, Spencer, you watch that charm of yours or you'll give me ideas." She attempted a little flirtatious batting of her stiffly mascaraed lashes but ended up coughing again, spewing a cloud of smoke in Georgia's face. Georgia sneezed.

"Is my smoke bothering you, honey?"

"Yes, Mrs. Hawkins, I'm afraid it is."

"Oh, dear." Eloise looked sympathetic, waving the air in front of her before taking another drag.

Spencer caught Georgia's eye, his mouth twitching with amusement. When she gave him what she hoped was a dirty look, he winked at her, his smile deepening the grooves running down his lean cheeks.

Georgia stared. The man was too damn good looking for his own good. And he knew how to use it. He had just used it with good effect on Eloise Hawkins, and the silly woman had eaten it up with a spoon. He had used it Friday night on her very own daughter—and he was trying to use it on her now. But just because the daughter had fallen for it, didn't mean the mother would. Looking into those navy-blue eyes, Georgia swore to herself that she wouldn't—swore very hard, while her insides did a little dance and her face felt a little hot.

The smile froze on Spencer's face. God, she was blushing. Fresh color stained her pale skin and she suddenly looked very pretty. Had he never winked at her before? Surely he had. Maybe he had just never noticed her reaction before. Lately he was noticing too damn much about Georgia Moon.

She wore one of her usual suits today but, remembering the glimpse of dewy skin peeking out from beneath her white robe Friday night, he was acutely aware of what was under it. The sophisticated little black number she'd worn to the gallery was hardly revealing and not all that sexy, but it had hinted at curves, just as her eyes had hinted at hunger. And now this blush—something that, no matter how prim and straight-backed she sat there, she could do nothing to hide.

A cloud of smoke from Eloise's cigarette floated between them, and Georgia sneezed again.

"Umm, look, Eloise, why don't we finish this out on the patio."

Once outside, Georgia leaned against the railing, pad in hand, but she had stopped listening. It was so hot, the hottest May she could remember in a long time. She put down her pad and unbuttoned her jacket, slipping it off, turning around to raise her face to the breeze coming off the lake. It felt good. She unbuttoned the top few buttons of her shirt, pulling the wilted material away from her damp flesh. Her fingers trailed across her skin, and the feeling she'd had the other morning came back, stronger than before. She wanted her clothes off, her body free. She could almost feel the cooling breeze on her breasts, her nipples hardening at the thought. An ache started in the pit of her belly, radiating a languid kind of heat, and she sighed—

Eloise Hawkins's voice brought her crashing back to earth.

"Listen, Spencer honey, you get me that hot tub and I'll be happy to share. Arthur's always off on some business trip, so there'll be plenty of room."

Georgia stiffened, disgusted at the barely veiled proposition, disgusted that a member of her gender would so easily fall for all that false Foxworth charm. But was she any different? One look from him, one innocent wink, and she was blushing like a schoolgirl, thinking wild thoughts again, longing for things she thought she'd left behind a lifetime ago.

It was all her mother's fault. She was the one who'd put the idea of going after Spencer into Georgia's head. She was the one who'd made her start thinking of him in a different light. Georgia had been immune to him for ten long years; she had absolutely no intention of succumbing to Foxworth fever now.

SPENCER WAS BENT OVER his worktable when Georgia gathered her things and quietly made her way to the door.

"George?"

With her hand still on the knob, she closed her eyes and swallowed, praying she wouldn't start blushing again, praying he wouldn't try to kiss her.

"Come over here a minute," he said softly, and she had no choice but to go. He swiveled on his work stool to face her. "There's something I've been wanting to ask you." He took her hand, pulling her closer until she stood between his knees. With his other hand, he fingered the lapel of her jacket, now safely back on her body where it belonged.

He had touched her like this before; it was one of the things he did to tease her and make fun of her, laughing at her when she got all blustery and pushed him away. The trouble was, this time she kept seeing him as he'd looked that morning, fresh from the lake, naked. She stared at the deep V opening of his shirt and imagined his skin, cool and slick with water, the flesh over his muscles beaded, dripping—

"You know that crazy group of architects I belong to—the one that meets twice a year?"

She forced her gaze off his chest and looked down to where he held her hand. His thumb moved rhythmically over her knuckles, back and forth, back and forth. She pulled her hand away. "The T-Squares," she said in a businesslike voice that almost caught in her throat.

He watched her mouth. Did he imagine the slight huskiness in her voice? "Yeah," he finally said, looking away, crossing his arms to keep from touching her again. "Well, it's my turn to host the party, and they're not going to let me worm my way out of it this time. I was thinking—most of the guys are married now and their wives will be here, too, so I need a hostess."

"You want me to act as hostess for the party?"

His eyes were on her mouth again—he couldn't seem to help it. Soft, pouty, inviting. He nodded. "Maybe after the party, we could go for a drive, have dinner in the country somewhere," he murmured, thinking aloud, his mind wandering to starlight, dark roads, cool night winds messing up that honey hair....

He uncrossed his arms, moved his hands to her waist, edging her closer. If he could just taste her—just touch his mouth to hers again—

"Sure, why not," those delectable lips said, all business, all trace of huskiness gone. "Of course, I'll expect my usual rate of pay."

Spencer dropped his hands and cleared his throat. "Of course."

"Fine. Just let me know how many to expect, and I'll call the caterer. Good night."

He watched her walk briskly to the door. Foxworth, he thought, you need your head examined. He looked down at his lap. And a very, very cold shower.

Chapter Five

Georgia arrived home, hot and tired, her throat parched from the incessant May heat wave and the traffic of a Milwaukee rush hour.

The house was dimly cool and seemingly deserted. She was grateful to find a pitcher of Jasmine's iced herbal tea in the refrigerator. The cold liquid stung her throat, but she quickly drained a glass, then pressed it to her forehead, sliding it back and forth against her sweat-sheened skin.

It was only when she put the glass down that she realized her hand was shaking.

He had teased her so many times, touched her so many times. But he'd never looked at her like he had that afternoon. There was something different in his eyes—those incredible navy eyes. A softness, a hesitancy.

Georgia shook herself. She was just being fanciful. This was Spencer Foxworth, the man for whom all of life was a game—a game he was used to winning. The thing that drove her crazy was that she wasn't sure what he was trying to win. Was he just buttering her up to get to Emily? Or— What was it he had said at the gallery? Something about it not being Emily he wanted.

What if he wanted *her?* What if his touch really *was* different this time? What if what she thought she saw in his eyes was real? What if, after all these years—

Her hand started shaking again. She could still feel the heat of his thighs, a mere whisper from her hips, still remember the deep tremor of his voice, the persuasive pull of his smile.

She quickly rinsed her glass at the sink, then walked to the back screen door. Jasmine stood at the far end of the yard, a large canvas on the easel in front of her. Even from this distance, Georgia could see the bright splashes of color that were her trademark. She pushed the door open, crossing the small back porch, descending the steps to walk across the grass. As she drew closer, the bold strokes took the shape of the weeping willow at the end of the yard. Jasmine had grouped several clay pots of geraniums on an old garden chair, shaded by the graceful fronds of the tree. A pair of gardening gloves and a trowel lay on the lawn as if the unseen gardener had just tossed them aside before leaving the picture.

As always, Jasmine's attention to her work blocked everything else from her mind, and Georgia stood watching unnoticed for several minutes.

"I wondered how long you would manage to stay away from it," she finally said.

Jasmine's hand and eyes never left the canvas. "I never can for long."

"It's lovely," Georgia murmured. She stood for several minutes more, watching her mother's intense concentration. Then she left her, walking slowly back to the house.

She went upstairs to take a shower, thinking that the house was empty. But when she passed Emily's door, the girl was inside, tossing things from her closet.

The room was a mess. Brightly colored clothes lay everywhere. Boxes of memorabilia, sketchbooks and photo albums were strewn across the bed. Georgia stood in the doorway, uneasy in the face of all this industry.

"Spring cleaning?" she asked a little too brightly.

"Oh—Mom. I didn't hear you come in."

Georgia strolled into the room, picking up a dried corsage from one of the boxes. Junior prom and Emily defiantly wearing something black and almost indecently short. She put the corsage down and picked up a handful of buttons, turning them over in her palm. Save the Dolphins—Don't Eat Tuna.

Greenpeace for a Green Earth. Pro-choice *Is* Pro-life.

Why had she denied how very much like Jasmine her daughter had always been? And why had she thought that homemade cookies and ruffled curtains could ever change that? This latest rebellion of dropping out of school was only another in a long line of rebellions.

She let the buttons drop from her fingers. "Dare I hope that you're packing to go back to school?"

Emily finished folding a sweater, smoothing the soft knit with deliberate care before answering. "You can hope anything you want, Mom, but it will just be a waste of time. I wish you would see that."

Georgia sighed and sat on the edge of the bed. "What are you doing, then?"

"I'm moving out."

Georgia was on her feet again in a shot. "You're *what?*"

"I've rented a small studio above the gallery where I've been working. There's enough room for a bed. I'm going to live there."

"You can't!"

"Yes I can—I am."

"But what will you live on? How can you afford it? If you think that I—"

Emily laughed. "No, Mom, don't worry. I'm not asking for a handout. I've got enough to live on for a while."

Georgia glanced toward the window where she could see Jasmine packing up her paints. "This is your grandmother's doing, isn't it? She's giving you the money."

Emily threw up her arms in exasperation, letting them fall hard to slap against her thighs. "Just stop blaming Jasmine for everything, will you? The money's mine," she added more gently. "I sold a piece."

"You sold a piece of sculpture?"

"That's right. The one I've been working on for a year of vacations and holidays. I knew it was good—and I was right. It sold."

"But—but how much could you have gotten for it? Surely not enough to—"

When Emily told her, she thought she must have misunderstood. "You're not serious?"

"Completely. And don't look so surprised. I have talent, Mother. Just ask Jasmine. Just ask Spencer Foxworth."

"What has he got to do with this?"

"Everything. He's the one who bought it."

Georgia practically fell back onto the bed. That rat. That sneaking, conniving slime. He'd spent the day flirting with Georgia, while all the while he knew what Emily was up to. All the while he'd been plotting to finance Emily's liberation, pay for a little bohemian love nest where he could come and go as he pleased.

"Really, Mother," Emily was saying, "you could take a few lessons from that gorgeous boss of yours. The man is a true liberal, laid-back—he knows how to enjoy life."

"Too bad he doesn't know how to act his age," Georgia muttered.

"Age has nothing to do with it, Mother. Some things are timeless."

"Yeah, like the playboy mentality. Emily, didn't you see the way the man was acting Friday night? Why, he almost—"

"You mean when he had you backed to the wall?" Emily laughed. "Come on, Mom, when you look like Spencer, flirting is a prerequisite to breathing. He probably learned it in the womb or something."

Georgia stared at her daughter, mouth open, poised to say more. But what was the use? Emily obviously thought her mother was no competition. She was totally secure in how Spencer felt about her. So secure that seeing him flirt with another woman gave her no reason to pause.

And why shouldn't she be secure? After all, the man had just financed a year of freedom for her. And he obviously intended to stick around to enjoy the fruits of his generosity.

THE STING of the pulsating shower massage beat down on Georgia as she swore under her breath, cursing Spencer Foxworth. How dare he buy her daughter!

Georgia grabbed the loofah and scrubbed at her body with a vengeance. To think she had almost fallen for all that studied charm! Well, he wasn't going to get away with it! What had Jasmine said? The right woman could make him forget all about seducing Emily. Yes, and by God, she was going to be that right woman, or kill herself trying. She'd lead him on a dance he'd never forget and then she'd expose him to Emily for what he really was. A user of women, an untrustworthy cad, a—a—

Soap flew from the loofah, hitting Georgia in the eye, stinging like hell. Blindly she groped for a towel, blaming Spencer Foxworth for this, too.

Out of the shower, she threw on her clothes, tugged a brush through her hair and ran down the stairs to find her mother.

Jasmine was in the kitchen, doing something disgusting with tofu and the alfalfa sprouts that she grew in jars on the kitchen window sill.

"Dump that mess down the disposal, Mother. You're coming with me."

"I am? Do you mind telling me where we're going, my love?"

"Shopping, Mother. We're going shopping. I've decided that since my life is taking on such a drastic change, maybe my wardrobe should, too."

Jasmine had the grace to look a little guilty. "Emily told you." She sighed and turned back to her sprouts. "I'm sorry, Georgia. I tried to get her to talk to you about it, but—"

"Forget it, Mother. It's already old news," Georgia answered briskly, taking Jasmine by the arm and hauling her away from the sink.

Jasmine didn't hide her surprise. "Are you sure you want me to go shopping with you, Georgia? You know we never see eye to eye on anything and always end up arguing."

"I've recently been led to believe that my sense of style could use a little help, so I'm prepared to let you win a few arguments. Tell you what—we'll compromise. I'll show you a great place to get a nice, greasy cheeseburger served with a mountain of fries and you can show me how to dress for success."

Jasmine looked surprised. "But, Georgia, don't you think you have enough power suits? Besides, I'd hardly be the one to advise you on business attire."

"Not business success, Mother—man success. I'm out to outfox a Foxworth, and you're going to show me how to bait the trap!"

THE MALL WAS NEARLY deserted, save for some people sitting around the fountain, soaking up the air-conditioning. Walking past them, Georgia wondered if that was how she'd end up— nothing better to do on a May evening than sit on a bench, alongside an artificial pond, breathing the artificial atmosphere, watching the world go by.

By the time they reached the dress shop, she was almost glad to be embarking on an adventure.

Their arms laden with clothes, they took the large corner dressing room, big enough for them to share. This kind of shopping was new to Georgia. She usually shopped for clothes twice a year, choosing one new suit in the spring, one in the fall. They were all much the same: black, brown, navy for winter; mauve, tan and lighter blue for spring and summer. She had built quite a wardrobe of them since they never seemed to go out of style—chiefly because they had no style.

Her casual wardrobe was nonexistent. Ancient shorts and T-shirts for summer, mainly sweats for the rest of the year, and a few pairs of tailored pants that went with several of the suit jackets. Nothing trendy, nothing sexy and certainly nothing just for fun.

Tonight, with Jasmine's help, she was out to change all that. For the first time in her life, she was glad she had a mother who didn't know how to dress her age, who didn't always follow all the rules and who wasn't afraid to take chances. Georgia only hoped it wasn't too late for her to learn a few things from Jasmine that she probably should have learned long ago.

"What do you think?" she asked her now, displaying a pair of white gauze trousers with matching jacket.

Jasmine halted in the middle of zipping up a denim jumpsuit. "I say lose the jacket."

"Really?" Georgia slipped the jacket off, revealing a shirt printed in tropical splendor.

"Now you're talking," said Jasmine. "You've got a nice bottom, George. Show it off a little."

The pants were tailored to hug her bottom, flowing out from her hips, barely skimming her legs, then tapering in again to end just at her ankles. Georgia twisted this way and that, fairly pleased with what she saw. "But this shirt—you can see right through it."

"That's what camisoles are for, love. Let me fetch you one."

Jasmine glided out of the fitting room, this time resplendent in a calf-length skirt, splashed with flowers, and a washed silk shirt. Georgia watched her go, admiring her comfort in walking among a bunch of strangers, barefoot and in clothes that weren't her own.

When she returned, her arms were full of more than just a camisole. She had scooped up other things for Georgia to try on, things a heck of a lot more daring than Georgia had picked for herself.

"What on earth—" Georgia held up a black halter top with a built-in bra beneath its daring sweetheart neckline.

"If you must wear suit jackets in the summer, that—" Jasmine pointed at the garment "—is what you should be wearing under them."

Georgia held it up in front of her. "You can't be serious? Mother, I'm hardly Marilyn Monroe."

Jasmine considered this. "No. She's dead, and you, my love, are alive. If you're going after Spencer Foxworth, you're going to need to pull out the heavy artillery. You've got breasts—use them."

Georgia wiggled into the halter, then faced herself in the mirror. Not bad—not bad at all. Maybe it had been a mistake to try to hide her full figure all these years.

Absolutely nothing was hidden in the scrap of black. Her creamy breasts swelled over the curve of the sweetheart neckline, making the most of every inch. It hugged her midriff, ending at the waist. Daring, sassy, crazy. And that's how it was making her feel. For the first time in her life, she felt all woman. Maybe even woman enough for Spencer Foxworth.

"Mother, I hate to admit it, but I think you may be right about this top."

"I may be right about a lot of things."

Georgia pulled the halter over her head and reached for her own clothes. "Come on, let's pay for this stuff and get going. You still have to find me the perfect dress for Spencer's party. I want something that will knock him off his feet."

"And onto his back?" Jasmine asked with deceptive innocence.

Georgia stopped buttoning her shirt and looked at her reflection in the mirror. Her hair was mussed, her face flushed, alive. Is that where this was headed—getting Spencer Foxworth into bed? Would she let it go that far? Would she have to? But another question seemed to linger, just outside her brain, trying to edge its way inside. And that question was: Did she want it to?

"VIN? ANYBODY HOME?"

Spencer rapped his knuckles against the new oak screen door of Vinnie Prescott's east-side Victorian. Light from a television screen flickered through the bowed living room window. The stentorian crescendo of old horror-movie music kept time with the dancing shadows.

Shirtless, Vinnie came around the corner from the living room, surprise registering on his face. "Spence, I didn't know you were coming over tonight."

"Neither did I. I was just driving around and I thought— Am I interrupting something?" He glanced into the living room and saw what he was interrupting. Emily Moon sat cross-legged on the floor in front of an empty pizza carton.

"Hi, Pops." She grinned, wiggling her fingers at him.

"Well, Emily—hello," Spence said, turning to Vinnie, who was looking decidedly sheepish.

"You're a little late for pizza. How about a beer?"

Spencer raised his brows. "You sure?"

"Sure. Come on."

Spencer followed Vinnie into the kitchen. "How long has this been going on?" he asked.

Vinnie shrugged. "She just called me up out of the blue. We got to talking, and the next thing I know I'm picking her up, bringing her back here and ordering pizza."

"Guess I've got lousy timing."

"Naw—we really were just watching TV."

Spence gave him a look.

"Really, man. Hey, I never pretended to be the lady's man you are, old buddy." Vinnie retrieved a beer from the refrigerator and handed it to Spencer.

"Yeah, well, suddenly being a lady's man doesn't look all that good."

"Your past come back to haunt you?"

Spence took a swig of beer and leaned against the counter. "Something like that." He told Vinnie about asking Georgia to be his hostess. "She totally misunderstood me. Said she'd be glad to do it for her usual rate of pay."

Vinnie gave a bark of laughter. "Not what you had in mind, huh?"

"Hell, no. I had a little moonlight in mind. A little soft, after-party seduction. A little—" Vinnie was shaking his head. "What?"

"Georgia Moon isn't that kind of woman, Spence. After ten years, you oughta know that."

Spencer put his half-finished beer down on the counter and ran his hands through his hair. "I know, I know. So how come I can't stop thinking about what she'd be like as that kind of woman? How come every time I look at her, I seem to see something I missed before? How come I can't get her out of my mind?"

Vinnie laughed, shaking his head. "Spence," he said, giving Spencer a slap on the back, "did you ever think that maybe you've finally met the woman who can clip your wings?"

"What do you mean?"

"Maybe it's love, old pal. Maybe it's love."

Motionless, Spencer stared at him, then shook himself, as if coming out of a stupor. "And maybe it's lust," he threw back. "Maybe it's just been too long between women."

The sound of Emily's laughter flowed from the living room. Both men looked toward the doorway.

"Don't even think it, Foxworth," Vinnie warned.

"Emily? Are you kidding? I'm old enough to be her father."

Vinnie choked on his beer. "You must have it bad, man. I mean, I *never* heard you say anything like that before."

Spencer laughed, shaking his head. "God, Vinnie, how could I be falling in love with Georgia Moon? The woman totally disapproves of me."

Vinnie slapped him on the back again. "Hell, Foxworth, I've never known you to back down from a challenge."

"A challenge? Hell, Vin, it would take a miracle."

Vinnie laughed again, hitting Spencer one more time on the back. "Or a hell of a lot of compromise," he said before going back to the living room and Emily.

The word ran around in Spencer's mind. *Compromise.* Something he'd never been very good at. Something he'd never wanted to be very good at. Something he'd vowed to leave behind once he'd broken away from his family. It'd have to be a pretty special woman to make him break that vow.

By the time Spencer followed Vinnie out to the living room, he was standing at the front door with Emily. She was looking up at him like he was some kind of white knight, accepting his chaste little good-night kiss, then leaning in for more before turning to Spencer.

"Spencer, if you're taking off, I'll cop a ride with you," she said brightly.

Spencer pushed past them, escaping out the screen door and down the stairs to wait on the front walk. He was jealous as hell. Not jealous of Emily and Vinnie together. No. Jealous because Georgia was never going to look at him that way. Jealous because he was never going to get the chance to kiss her like that, in front of God and man and the moths circling the porch light. He still remembered the sting of the resounding slap she'd given him when he'd tried to nearly ten years ago.

Was Vinnie right? Was he ready to have his wings clipped? Was he falling in love with Georgia Moon?

THE JAG PULLED UP in front of Georgia's Cape Cod. Spence ducked his head, trying to see if any lights were on.

"Looking for someone?" Emily asked coyly.

"Just wondering if your mother was still up."

"Oh, she'll be up, all right. She always waits up. Want to come in?"

He looked at Emily, then back at the house. Yeah, maybe he'd come in. Have a cup of coffee. Talk to Georgia, get her to see another side of him—if another side existed. Then he remembered that white robe. Then he remembered that falling for a woman like Georgia Moon was not where he wanted to be. *Was* it?

"Well?"

Emily was waiting for an answer. "No—better not. I've got work to do."

Emily shrugged. "Okay. Thanks for the ride, Pops. See ya."

Spencer sat in the Jag watching Emily bounce up the front steps. This was a fine state of affairs. He was taking the beautiful young girl home, yes, but she was calling him Pops and inviting him in to see her mother. He pulled the Jag away from the curb, heading for the corner, thinking the worst of it was that it was the mother and her damn, pristine white robe he couldn't get out of his mind.

THE WARM EVENING BREEZE drifted in the window, stirring the lace curtains, stirring Georgia's senses. She stood in her bedroom, staring at the reflection in the mirror above her dresser. She had never looked like this in her life.

The soft, sheer chiffon layers of the ivory dress Jasmine had chosen for her floated around her body, softly outlining curves, showing hints of the silk chemise under it all. The neckline scooped low and loose over her breasts, baring just a glimpse, hinting at far more. The thin straps, covered with crystals, rested widely spaced on her shoulders. The hemline floated near midcalf, but the chemise stopped earlier, letting the shadow of leg peek through.

The dress shifted in the breeze, caressing her skin—sensual, exciting. What would Spencer think when he saw her in it? Would he look at her like he looked at other women—like she'd never been looked at by a man before? She closed her eyes, imagining his touch, imagining—

The sound of a car engine drifted in through the open window, stopping out in the street below. Georgia opened her eyes. Something about the sound was familiar, and she padded to the window in bare feet to peer out.

Spencer's Jag was parked across the street, the engine still running. Had she conjured him up, imagining his touch? What was he doing here?

The passenger door opened and out bounced Emily. Georgia ducked behind the lace curtain. That rat!

She stomped back over to the mirror. Yes, the dress would do and she'd wear it and go as far as she had to. She'd knock Spencer on his back and out of Emily's reach. And she would never again forget that this was war, and the dress draping her body, stirring her senses, was a weapon.

Chapter Six

Spencer came in from a morning walk on the beach to find a strange woman in his living room. And what a woman. She had her back to him so he couldn't see her face, but her body...

The white trousers she wore hugged her curvy bottom and the morning sun streamed through them, outlining her long, shapely legs and trim ankles. Suddenly the woman turned and Spencer found himself staring at a sheer, tropical print shirt worn over something silky and brief.

The woman started walking toward him, her full breasts moving gently, her hips swaying with her confident stride.

Now, here was a woman who could get his mind off Georgia. Here was a woman who could get his mind off almost anything—

"Water too cold for a swim this morning?" she asked, and his gaze flew to her face. That voice—

Good Lord—it *was* Georgia.

But not *his* Georgia. This Georgia's skin was somehow brighter, her hair bouncier, her lips fuller, more inviting, her eyes smoky, deeper—eyes he could get lost in.

Eyes he *was* getting lost in.

"Holy cow," he murmured. "I mean—wow. It's you. I mean—" His eyes fed, his mind whirled, his body reacted.

He quickly turned away from her, embarrassed, stunned—and hotter than hell.

He was acutely aware of her following behind him all the way to his worktable, her provocative, spicy scent drifting over his shoulder and straight to his nostrils.

"No swim this morning?" she repeated.

"Um—no. Uh, I decided to take a long walk instead," he stammered, sliding onto his work stool, thinking that a swim in ice-cold Lake Michigan was probably just what he needed.

"Are you feeling all right?" She placed a hand gently on his forehead, a miraculously cool, soft hand. "It's not like you to skip your morning dip."

Her hand skimmed over his forehead, her fingers brushing his hair, then skittering over his ear until finally just the tip of one finger traced his jawline.

The whole action took maybe two seconds, but Spencer experienced it in slow motion, seeing the tip of that finger, painted jungle pink, come to rest on Georgia's lower lip after its sensual journey.

"We have nothing pressing going on this morning, so if you've changed your mind, there's still plenty of time for a dip."

Maybe *she* had nothing pressing, but he definitely did. There was no way he was getting into a swimsuit in his condition. Hell, there was no way he was *standing up* in his condition.

She leaned closer. "Are these the schematics for the Hawkins house?"

"Umm, yeah—" Her breast brushed his arm and he gripped his pencil tighter to keep himself from pulling her into his arms and finding out if she was as soft as she looked.

"Interesting—I'm sure Eloise will be pleased."

He let out his breath in relief when she finally moved away. But the click of her heels drew his senses, and he couldn't stop himself from taking a look. Turquoise high-heeled sandals, baring her toes—toes painted the same jungle pink as her fingers. His gaze moved up her long, long legs. Good Lord, how was he going to get any work done today?

By midmorning, he was wondering why he was bothering to try. Why didn't he just take her into his arms and taste those lips he couldn't seem to get his mind off of? How was he supposed to keep his mind on floor plans and perspectives with her clicking across the oak floor of his wall-less house? Had she always moved around so much during a workday? Had her hips always swayed like that? And had she always found as many excuses to interrupt his work, to lean over his shoulder, to brush his body with her own?

From any other woman, he would have interpreted a dozen invitations since he'd walked in from the patio that morning. From Georgia Moon, he didn't know what to make of it. With any other woman, he would have satisfied his curiosity by now—grabbed her, kissed her and found out just what was on her mind. With Georgia, he didn't know what to do.

Suspicion somehow kept niggling away at his brain. What was she up to? Why the big change? Was she trying to get him to make a pass just so she could flatten him again? Did she have some hidden agenda, some reason he couldn't fathom for wanting to drive him crazy? Because by the middle of the afternoon, that's exactly where he was headed—crazy.

She wiggled and clicked over to him, carrying a sweating glass of iced tea. The tea wasn't the only thing sweating.

"You've been working so hard all day, Spencer. Why don't you take a break," she cooed, her fingers trailing slowly across the glass when she placed it before him, leaving a pattern in the condensation.

He stared at the drops of water coursing down the glass, undulating, curving. They reminded him of—

He grabbed the glass and took a long, hard swallow, almost choking when he felt her damp fingers at the back of his neck, ruffling through his hair, gently massaging.

He stood up abruptly, shuffling paper, refusing to look at her. He had to get out of there or he wasn't going to be responsible for what might happen.

"Yeah, I think you're right," he said, his voice gruff, abrupt. "I need a break. I probably won't be back till after you leave for the day. Lock up."

Spencer rushed for the door, practically knocking her over, getting one last teasing, tormenting whiff of her scent, one last brush of that delectable, soft, womanly body.

If he'd been lusting after her before, in her prim, buttoned-up blouses and sexless business suits, now, with her high heels and soft clothes outlining her lush curves, he was in an agony of desire. And he had absolutely no idea what to do about it.

GEORGIA WAS IN a different kind of agony. She felt completely foolish and way out of her depth. All day, she'd done her best to jiggle and click, to brush and touch, to no avail. Spencer seemed to actually pay *less* attention to her than usual.

Rubbing cold cream on her face, trying to obliterate the totally useless makeup, she suddenly stopped, an infuriating possibility entering her mind. What if Spencer actually thought she had fallen for him? What if he actually thought she was out to ensnare him, not to keep him away from Emily—he was obviously too obtuse and egotistical to come to that conclusion—but because after ten years she'd succumbed to his charms and now had a major case of the hots for him? He had certainly acted like a man scared off by a woman's romantic designs. He'd made his midafternoon escape fast and furiously, nearly knocking her over trying to get away from her.

The idea that he might think she actually wanted him made her mad enough to spit. And maybe she would have, but she'd probably blow a gob of cold cream right in her eye. She finished wiping the greasy stuff off her face and stomped back to her bedroom.

"Give it up, Georgia," she muttered, "before you make a complete fool of yourself." She opened her closet door and started to yank her new clothes off the hangers. Most of them still had the tags hanging from them; they'd be easy enough to return. And that's exactly what she was going to do. Return the whole lot and go back to treating Spencer Foxworth like the cad he was.

The phone jangled, but before she could cross the floor to answer it, it stopped. Must have been for Emily, she reasoned, hearing the muffled peal of her daughter's laughter through the open bedroom door. Georgia glanced at the clock. It was late. Emily seemed to be getting a lot of late-night calls lately.

And there was that teasing laughter again. Suspicion pushing her, Georgia's hand reached for the phone.

No, she thought, stopping her hand mid-air—she couldn't. She couldn't blatantly listen in on Emily's phone call. She hadn't sunk that low—not yet.

But she could just casually stroll down the hall, perhaps pause at Emily's door.

Quietly, she made her way into the hall. If she stood very still and very close to Emily's closed door, she could just make out her words.

"Of course you're not too old for me," she was saying. "I happen to like older men." She laughed again. "Yes, last night was fun, and yes, I'd like to do it again."

Georgia's mouth dropped open. She didn't need to hear any more. Scurrying back to her own room, she carefully shut the door behind her.

Was that Spencer on the phone with Emily? Who else could it be? She'd seen Emily bouncing out of the Jag last night. They'd been together. They'd had fun. *They were going to do it again!*

And now Georgia remembered hearing the phone ring the night before—late, while she'd been busy painting her toenails. Just about half an hour after seeing Spencer drop Emily off. Just about long enough for him to make it home. He must have raced for the phone—the rat!

She paced her bedroom, chewing on a nail, cursing inwardly. Her head jerked up at the sound of Emily's laughter again. What could Spencer possibly be saying that was so damn funny? Because it had to be him. Didn't it? Unless, of course, Emily had another older man tucked away somewhere.

Georgia stopped pacing. Was it possible that there was someone else and she was wrong? Her mind streamed through several possibilities—all of them preferable to Spencer.

In fact, *anyone* was preferable to Spencer.

But, of course, none of them were as likely as Spencer. None of them as good looking, as charming, as sexy—

Georgia grabbed the pile of new clothes she'd thrown on the bed and started to put them back on the hangers. She was going to choose the most flamboyant, the most sexy of the lot, and she was going to wear it tomorrow. Because Spencer Foxworth wasn't going to get away with it. He wasn't going to perform pillow talk with her daughter all night, making plans to do it again. Whatever *it* was.

She was going to put a stop to *it,* even if she had to make a fool out of herself!

SPENCER WAITED at his worktable like a man awaiting execution. It couldn't possibly be as bad as the day before. Could it? Surely this morning Georgia would show up in her usual sexless suit, prim shirt and sensible one-and-a-half-inch heels. He felt like he was being asked to undergo some torturous test. Look but don't touch. Want but don't take.

At least, he didn't think he was supposed to touch or take. Could it be that Georgia, after all these years— Naw. She had just bought some new clothes, that was all. She probably had absolutely no idea what effect she could have on a man. She'd always been a little innocent under that prickly exterior.

Spencer picked up his pencil and started to sketch. Yeah, today she'd show up looking more like the old Georgia, and by the end of the day he will have forgotten all about her painted toes peeking out of those high, sexy sandals. He will have forgotten all about the sweet curve of her bottom in those gauze pants. And he would definitely not remember the rise and fall of her full breasts under that silky little thing she wore under her transparent shirt.

The door opened behind him. "Good morning," he heard her call out in a voice laced with honey. He swiveled on his stool, peering through the fretwork of the shelves that separated him from temptation.

And temptation it was. Spencer groaned. It was worse—much worse—than yesterday.

Georgia wore a pair of black leggings, molded to her shapely legs, topped with a sheer dotted shirt over something that hugged her midriff and dipped dangerously low over the lush curve of her breasts. His gaze flew to her feet. She wore flats this time— thank God. It wasn't much of a concession, but it was something, at least.

He'd thought to turn around again, get back to work before she noticed him staring. But she started toward him and it was too late.

Her breasts jiggled when she moved, the open shirt flapping behind her, her generous curves lovingly caressed by form-fitting knit. He couldn't take his eyes off her. He didn't *want* to take his eyes off her.

His pencil snapped in two in his hands and fell to the floor. He bent to pick it up, and by the time he straightened, she was standing just inches in front of him. He got a good, long, close look all the way up. That is, until he smacked his forehead soundly on the corner of the table. Stars burst in his brain.

"Spencer, my goodness, are you all right?" Georgia wanted to cringe at the sugar in her own voice, but it seemed to be working. His eyes were riveted to her, his face flushed under his tan. "Oh,

Spencer, I'm afraid you're going to have a nasty bump.'' She touched her fingers lightly to the spot, making soothing noises, then she curled her hand around his neck and tilted his head down to kiss it better.

Spencer went instantly hard at the touch of her mouth. What was she trying to do to him? Whatever it was, she wasn't finished. Her eyes moved over his face, her lips parted, she moved closer—

And then she was kissing him full on the mouth, like she couldn't help herself, like she wanted him as much as he wanted her. He held still for one stunned moment, then his mouth opened against hers and he was kissing her back.

Georgia knew the moment she'd lost control of the kiss, knew the moment her heartbeat changed, her pulse quickened, her bones turned to water. It was dazzling—but it was a mistake.

She pulled away.

But Spencer wanted more. He started to pull her closer—

She stiffened. ''What are you doing?'' she gasped.

His eyes narrowed, but he didn't let go of her. ''The question, George, is what are *you* doing?''

Her brows rose innocently. ''What do you mean?''

He looked down at her breasts. "The clothes, the kiss—what gives? Where's my prim-and-proper Georgia?"

She forced herself to give him a coy little smile. "Don't you like the new Georgia?"

His hands moved up and down her arms and she bit her bottom lip, trying not to shiver.

"Oh, sweetheart, I like her all right. I'm just not sure what to do with her. Every message I'm getting says she likes me, too."

"Well, maybe she does," she answered shyly, placing a hand on his chest, trying to act overcome with sudden attraction. But the way her heart was pounding, she wasn't sure how much of an act it was anymore.

"After ten years of put-downs? Come on, George, what's going on? What do you really want?"

Her gaze lingered over his face. His incredibly blue eyes, sparkling with heat; the chestnut hair falling rakishly over his forehead; the sculpted lips, lips she now knew somehow felt soft and firm at the same time; and that damn sexy cleft in his chin. "Maybe I want you," she murmured, her voice soft, husky, surprising to her own ears. Such an actress—

"You keep looking at me like that, George, and you just might have me."

Before she could say anything, his mouth came down on hers. The kiss was even more potent this time because he was in charge from the first. He'd taken her by surprise and her gasp parted her lips enough for his tongue to slide in and dance around. He was thorough, he was expert. She tried to hang on to that thought, the thought that he was expert because he'd done it millions of times before, with millions of women—her own daughter included. But the thought kept getting fractured, melting away with the rest of her body. Finally she moaned and pushed him away.

He reached for her again, but she stepped back. "Don't—don't you have to go out to the site today? Didn't Vinnie call about some problem yesterday?"

Shaken, Spencer ran his hands through his hair. Was she running cold on him again? She certainly didn't look cold. Her face was flushed, her mouth a little swollen, and her breathing was doing tormenting things to the getup she had on. He'd gotten to her—he'd be willing to bet on it. But why had she let him?

He took a deep breath. "Yeah, I do. Guess I better get out there." He gave her one last look before heading for the door. It was just as well, he thought. He'd get no work done with her jiggling around all day. He could use a breather. He needed time to think, to sort this whole thing out.

At the door he turned. A mistake. She looked so damn desirable—those sexy clothes and that innocent, puzzled look on her face.

"Come with me," he said.

Georgia's heart nearly stopped. Dare she go with him? She was supposed to be in control of the situation, but he had taken over far too easily. Still, at least she'd made some progress. At least he was no longer immune to her efforts. Wasn't that exactly what she wanted?

"Okay," she said, knowing that if her plan was going to work, she had to press on.

He smiled and held out his hand. She went to him, but didn't touch him. She wouldn't touch him again until she had herself back under complete control, otherwise her traitorous female body might make her forget that it was only a game.

SPENCER TRIED to keep his eyes on the road, but every nerve of his being registered Georgia's movements. He imagined the rising of her breast as she lifted the sun-kissed hair off her neck. In his mind, he saw the sheer shirt she wore billow out from her body, allowing the hot wind to caress her skin. He saw before him not the winding road of the shores of Lake Michigan, but smooth, narrow feet with well-shaped toes and their tantalizing pink tips.

Maybe she wanted him—that's what she had said. Then she had pulled away. But when he'd asked, nearly implored her, to come along, she'd accepted. If she had deliberately set out to drive him crazy, she couldn't have done a better job.

Spencer pulled the Jag into the gravel drive and the air was immediately cooler. The lot was heavily wooded, the trees, in leafy May splendor, providing a canopy that filtered the sun, casting dappled shadows against the car's gleaming surface.

"Mmm, this is wonderful—so cool and shaded."

"It's a beautiful piece of land. Stan and Maddy were lucky to find it. There's not much lake frontage available this close to the city." Spence pulled into the gravel turnaround just in front of the house he'd designed for the Murdochs. Nearly finished, it sat squarely on its wooded lot, three stories high. Very few windows faced the drive, and these were set horizontally, long and narrow, obviously high off the floor.

Georgia got out of the car, leaning against it, surveying everything in silence. Spence opened his door and slowly slid out. He crossed his arms over the top of the open car door, bracing himself, his eyes on Georgia.

Beyond bullying him into meeting deadlines and urging him to get going on new projects, she never took much interest in his work, visiting sites only when it was necessary for her to deliver amended plans or new drawings. Now he found himself anxiously waiting for her reaction, wanting her approval more than he cared to admit.

Leaves rustled overhead. Birds swooped and chirped shrilly, announcing the new arrivals, warning of their presence. The mossy, loamy scent of damp earth rose from the shaded ground.

Vinnie's truck and a few beat-up cars were parked ahead of them. Sounds came from inside the unfinished house—gruff voices calling to one another, the buzz of a saw, the whine of a drill. But for Spencer, nothing existed, nothing but the sight of Georgia's sun-dappled face lifted to the structure he'd created from images pulled from his brain, the house that was a part of him as surely as his heart or his soul. He wanted her to like it, this woman he'd managed to keep from falling in love with for ten years. He wanted her to like it because he was very much afraid that he was falling in love with her now.

"Well, what do you think?" he finally asked.

"I'll let you know after I see the inside," she answered, starting toward the house.

Catching up with her, he swung her playfully around to face him. "You just love to leave a guy dangling, don't you?" His eyes narrowed and the smile dimmed on his mouth. "What kind of game are you playing, George?"

She shrugged, keeping her voice light, keeping her mind off the feel of his hands on her arms. "What makes you think I'm playing a game?"

"Oh, you're playing a game, all right, Ms. Moon." He jerked her up close to him, her breasts grazing his chest, his eyes watching her startled mouth. She wasn't as sure of herself as she pretended. "I just hope when you lose, you're going to be ready to pay up, because I'll be more than ready to collect."

When she shivered, she told herself it was the shade beneath the trees. "And if you lose?"

"You should know by now, George, I never lose."

She stood still for a moment, absorbing his words, a thrill going through her. Fear? Or just plain good old-fashioned lust? Was she going to swoon and pant every time he touched her? Because if she did, she would surely lose, even if she won.

She jerked away from him and headed for the house, throwing over her shoulder, "You may just have met your match, Foxworth. And don't call me George!"

Just then, Vinnie came around the side of the house. "Hey, Foxworth, am I glad to see you. Those kitchen cabinets are giving my guys troub—" His eyes lit on Georgia and he stopped dead.

To Spencer's surprise, he didn't much like the way Vinnie was noticing the change in Georgia, didn't like it at all. Could Vinnie be the reason Georgia had accepted his invitation so readily this time, when in the past she'd avoided visiting sites with him?

Spencer looked at the younger man. Georgia had said more than once that Vinnie was a nice guy— something she'd never accused Spencer of being. But, hell, the guy was years too young for her. Besides, there was Emily. Definitely more Vinnie's type, more his age, more his speed. Vin was too easygoing to handle a woman like Georgia. Hell, Spence was having enough trouble handling her himself.

No, George couldn't be after Vinnie. No way. But just in case, he was getting her out of Vin's way as soon as possible.

"Uh, let's take a look at those cabinets, Vin, while Georgia takes a look around."

Vinnie stood his ground. "Hey, no hurry, pal. I was just telling Georgia—"

"Come on." Spencer cut him off, feeling like a teenage sorehead. "Your time may not be valuable, but mine is."

Vinnie looked surprised, then shrugged and followed him into the house, holding the door for Georgia.

Spencer's trademark wall of glass brought the trees inside—maple, birch and fir. The grounds were thick with them, blocking any view of the lake. The rough wood planking covering the walls and the stone of the massive fireplace blended perfectly with nature's setting.

Georgia walked farther into the house. To her right was an open staircase, and she peered up it. The light seemed brighter up there, and she was eager to explore. One foot on the bottom step, she suddenly stopped, unsure if it was safe to go on.

She looked toward Spencer and Vinnie, their heads bent over a blueprint, a few workmen standing behind them, looking over their shoulders. She hated to call attention to herself by interrupting. In the end, the desire to see the rest of the house won out.

"Spencer," she called, "is it safe to go up?"

One by one, the men looked up from the blueprint. Spencer looked at Vinnie. "Vin?" he asked.

Vinnie nodded. "Sure, Georgia, go right ahead."

Four pairs of eyes watched her progress up the stairs until her legs disappeared on the second floor.

"Wow," said one of the men.

"Man, oh man," said the other.

"Okay, guys," Spencer growled, "show's over. Get back to work."

The men went back to their tools, grumbling good-naturedly.

"Man, Foxworth, how long has this been going on?" Vinnie asked.

"Since yesterday," Spencer answered, rubbing at the back of his neck. His muscles felt tight, stretched.

"Man, how do you get any work done?"

"For the most part, I don't," Spencer answered.

One of the men behind them laughed, and Spence gave a quick glance over his shoulder before leading Vinnie away, over to the fireplace.

"I don't know, Vin. It's like she's out to get me."

Vinnie laughed and shook his head. "You're paranoid, pal. The lady's got you paranoid."

"It's not just the clothes. She's coming on to me—flirting. One day she's snapping at me with that acid tongue of hers, the next day she's bringing me iced tea and jiggling around the office, showing off a body that—"

Vin patted him on the back. "Yeah, good buddy, I saw."

"And not only that—" he looked behind him again and lowered his voice "—this morning, she kissed me."

Vinnie grinned. "And?"

"And I kissed her back."

"And?" Vinnie prompted again.

"And wow."

"So what's the problem?"

Spencer glanced toward the staircase where Georgia had disappeared. "I don't know, Vin. I think the lady's playing games with me, but I can't figure out why."

Vinnie whacked him on the back. "Foxworth, you may just have met your match."

Spencer looked at him sharply. "That's weird. That's exactly what she just said."

Vinnie whacked him again. "Then I guess we're both right."

Chapter Seven

"Do you like it?" he asked.

She stood at the wall of windows on the third floor, her back to him. Even if she hadn't heard his footfalls on the stairs, she would have sensed his presence in this wonderful space he had created.

"It's beautiful," she answered truthfully. "It's like you designed the entire house to fit between the trees."

"I did. It's always been important to me as an architect to maintain the land as closely as possible to the way nature made it."

She felt him moving closer. Now that she'd allowed herself to see—really see—his work, recognize his talent and vision, she was nervous facing him. She'd always treated him like he was nothing but a playboy, earning a bogus reputation designing the same house over and over again. She had never allowed herself to see this side of him before.

And she wasn't sure if she wanted to see it now. It would be easier to go on thinking of him as nothing more than a problem she had to conquer, a quest she had to pursue. For Emily's sake.

He came up behind her, placing his hands at her waist. The accelerated beat of her heart had nothing to do with Emily.

Spencer pulled her back against him, hoping she'd settle into his arms, hoping she'd move her head just enough for him to kiss her. He wanted to feel her soft mouth under his, here, amid the smell of new wood, amid the skeleton of his creation. He inched his fingers along her midriff, his thumb skimming the soft underside of her breast. Opening his lips against her earlobe, he nibbled.

And Georgia almost lost it. Her body went liquid, flowing into his. Her breath came out in a sigh. Her breasts swelled, yearning. Just before she started to purr like an indulged tabby cat, she caught herself. Forcing a laugh, she whirled out of his arms.

"I know my job description is varied and unconventional, but I don't believe fondling among the sawdust is anywhere in there, Mr. Foxworth."

"Then it should be, Ms. Moon," he teased, reaching for her again.

She batted his hands away. "I believe taking me out for an expensive lunch *is* in there, though." Yes, thought Georgia, a nice, safe, crowded public place. Somewhere he'd have to keep his hands to himself no matter how outrageously she flirted. She flattened her hand against his chest, moving it up and down slowly, looking up at him with wide, teasing eyes. "How about it, boss?"

Spencer had all he could do to remember that it was only lunch she was proposing. He grabbed her hand, stilling its teasing caress. "Lunch isn't really what I'm hungry for," he murmured. "But it's a start."

THE RESTAURANT, on Milwaukee's Old World 3rd Street, overlooked the river. The worst of the lunch crowd had gone and the place was quiet, the pace unhurried. They sat at a tiny table near the window. Outside, a Lake Michigan excursion boat, its pristine whiteness glaring in the strong sunlight, was moored at the pier to discharge the passengers from its lunch cruise. They were a tanned, well-heeled-looking lot. Their summer pastels blowing in the breeze, they mouthed words lost to the couple sitting in the cool dimness of the restaurant, as if the glass isolated them from another world, a world of noise and color.

That was the real world out there, Georgia reminded herself. It couldn't possibly be real in here, sitting across from this disturbing man, her knees almost touching his under the impossibly small table. She felt tension in every muscle as she tried to hold her body still so it wouldn't come in contact with his, tried to remember why she was there.

A cute little blond waitress came to take their order, obviously determined to display every one of her pearly little teeth for Spencer's benefit. Bending over to point out the day's specials on the menu, she let one of her perky little breasts brush his arm and giggled ridiculously when he merely asked a question about the clam chowder. She couldn't have been more obvious if she had lain down on a platter and presented herself as the entrée of the day.

Instead of being disgusted, Georgia was glad. It helped put things into perspective. This was the man who was after her daughter, the womanizer who liked them young. She'd known him for ten years. People didn't change, not overnight. She didn't know his reason for being there with her, but she knew her reason for being there with him. Emily. Back to business.

"I've hired a caterer for the party Friday night," Georgia told him when the waitress finally tore herself away. "It wasn't easy on such short notice, but I found a little company that does these wonderful cocktail kabobs with everything from shrimp to vegetables to fruit. I ordered a crisp semidry white wine that should go with everything, and your liquor cabinet is well stocked."

So, the efficient Ms. Moon was back, thought Spencer. He was aware that something had changed since they had entered the restaurant, but he didn't know what, and he didn't know why. He only knew that the woman who'd kissed him, the woman who'd touched him and teased him, was gone and the efficient and slightly difficult Ms. Moon was back. He sighed. "What about a bartender?" he finally asked.

"A bartender? For six couples? Come on, Spencer, you don't need a bartender for twelve people."

Spencer held up a finger. "Fourteen, counting you and me."

"Even so—" Georgia leaned farther over the table to make her point "—why waste money on a bartender? You and I can handle the first couple of rounds, and after that everyone can help themselves. The T-Squares aren't exactly black-tie, are they?"

Spencer hadn't heard a word since she'd leaned over the table. His eyes were riveted on all that soft flesh spilling forth from the little knit thing she wore under her open shirt. He imagined his tongue delving into the shadowy valley between her breasts, tasting her sun-warmed skin.

Georgia saw him looking, and her first inclination was to sit back in her chair and pull the shirt protectively around herself while making a cutting remark about male chauvinist pigs. But wasn't this why she'd bought these clothes in the first place? She leaned over still farther.

"Spencer, are you listening to this?" she purred, running a fingertip across the back of his hand where it rested on the table between them.

A bolt of lightning shot from his hand all the way down to his lower regions. What the woman could do with one little finger. But what had she said? With one last glance at that glorious pale flesh, he stammered, "Wha—what did you say?"

"I said, the T-Squares aren't exactly black-tie, are they?"

Spencer cleared his throat, careful to keep his eyes on her face. "Well—as a matter of fact, we do go black-tie."

"No kidding? Hmm—well." Georgia sat up straighter, withdrawing her finger from his hand. No need to go overboard. Besides, she could tell by the look on his face that she'd gotten her point across. "Even so," she said primly, "you can do without the expense of a bartender. No need to dip into the Foxworth trust fund for such a small party."

Spencer let out his breath, wondering if something was wrong with the restaurant's air conditioner. It felt decidedly warmer than it had a few minutes ago. What had they been talking about? Oh, right—his trust fund. "Well, I generally do like to reserve that money for things Granny Foxworth would disapprove of, and I'm afraid a black-tie cocktail party would be right up her alley."

And amateur modern art, sculpted by a young lady he was hoping to bed, wouldn't? Was that how he planned to get his hands on the money for Emily's sculpture without her knowing about it?

Georgia looked away from him, feigning a sudden interest in a speedboat shooting up the river, afraid she would blurt out something that would give the game away.

She had known about the Foxworth trust fund, of course, but she had no idea how large it was. Spencer never used that money for his regular living expenses; she wasn't even aware of who managed it for him. All she knew was that he came from an old family in San Francisco—an old family with old money.

In all the years she'd worked for him, he'd never visited his relatives, and none of them, if they existed, had ever visited him. Georgia, with her less than normal family background, had never thought it strange. She had always assumed that he was the black sheep. After all, Spencer would qualify for the black sheep in almost any family.

The waitress came with their seafood salads, and Georgia took some satisfaction in the girl's confusion at being so completely ignored by Spencer. If she let herself, she would be feeling decidedly smug. After all, she was forty years old and the man had been practically drooling. In fact, it had been criminally easy to distract him, despite the miniskirted waitress with the twenty-year-old body. Much too easy.

She peered suspiciously up at Spencer just in time to see a succulently large shrimp disappear between his moist lips. The man even chewed elegantly. Her eyes dropped to the cleft in his chin as she wondered irreverently what it would feel like to touch it with her tongue. Rough, perhaps salty— God, what was she doing?

She dipped her head and stared at her plate, pushing a chunk of crab around with her fork, suddenly having no appetite. He was supposed to be the one panting, not her. It wouldn't do to forget herself and go falling for the man, wouldn't do at all. And it would never happen. She was immune. Ten years of close proximity had provided her with a lot of antibodies, and it would take more than an appreciation of his talent, more than a pair of well-sculpted lips and a delicious little cleft, to make her succumb to Foxworth fever.

"Is something wrong with your salad, George?"

Georgia stabbed a piece of seafood with her fork, using more force than necessary, considering the shrimp was already a goner. "Why do you insist on calling me George even though I've asked you not to?"

"Why do you keep asking me not to?"

His tone was teasing, only making her inexplicably angrier. She moved her head impatiently. "It's bad enough having your parents name you after the state in which you were conceived without having it shortened to something ridiculously cutesy."

He picked up her hand. "If you don't want to be called something ridiculously cutesy, then maybe you should stop being so ridiculously cute."

"I *am not* cute. I'm mad."

He grinned. "So maybe you're cute when you're mad."

Georgia rolled her eyes. "Come on, Spencer, a free-spirited playboy like you should be able to come up with something more original than that."

He raised her hand to his lips. "Okay. How about, when I look into your fiery hazel eyes, words fail me, my mind turns to mush, my heart—"

Georgia burst out laughing. "Did Candy what's-her-name fall for that line?"

"Candy what's-her-name wasn't the hard sell that Georgia Moon is."

"Do something really unconventional, Spencer. Try good, old-fashioned, honest conversation for a change. And—"

"And?" Spencer asked, hopefully.

Georgia looked pointedly at the hand still holding hers. "And give me my hand back so I can eat this excellent seafood salad."

He raised her hand to his lips again, but instead of kissing it, he bit down softly on her knuckles. The

sensation went right through her. She snatched her
hand back and started to dig into her crabmeat.

"So you were conceived in the state of Georgia."

"Or so the story goes. Personally, I've never un-
derstood how they could be certain of that, since
they moved around so much. Still do for that matter—only now they do it separately."

"Divorced?" Spencer asked.

"My parents would never do anything as conventional as get a divorce. Actually, I think they still
love each other—they just can't stand to live together. Every couple of years they manage to end up
in the same place and have what I guess you could
call an *intra*marital affair."

Spencer chuckled. "Your childhood must have
been wild."

Georgia thought for a moment. "*Wild*'s a good
word."

"The exact opposite of mine."

"Really?"

Spencer nodded. "You've heard of the mother of
invention? Well, I was raised by Granny Foxworth,
the mother of *con*vention. I've been fighting the ties
that bind ever since I left home at the age of
twenty."

"So that's why you're determined never to settle
down."

Looking into those amber-sparked eyes, he could
feel that determination slipping. Maybe it had been

slipping little by little ever since she'd walked into his life ten years ago. "And that's why *you* were so determined *to* settle down."

She stared at him for a moment, then slowly started to smile. "We make quite a pair, don't we?"

He took hold of her hand again, rubbing his thumb slowly over her knuckles. "We could."

The man was rising to the bait like a brainless, ravenous fish. The only trouble was, Georgia was feeling pretty ravenous herself. That thumb grazing the back of her hand... Those dark blue eyes, like the center of a flame, creating heat along her skin... He was so different from any man she had ever known. Dangerous, exciting. Her whole life had been spent playing it safe. And what had it ever gotten her? A husband who cheated on her, a mother who didn't understand her, a daughter who was about to leave her. What was left for Georgia?

This man, sitting across from her? This man, touching her hand, making her heart leap and spin?

"Why don't we get out of here? Take a walk?"

"Shouldn't we be getting back to work? The messages are probably piling up."

"Hey, I'm the boss, remember? I'm giving you the afternoon off—on one condition."

Georgia raised a brow. "And that condition is?"

"You have to spend it with me."

Before she could give herself time to think, time to decide that it might be a mistake, Georgia turned her hand in his. "Mr. Foxworth," she said, "you've got yourself a deal."

They strolled up Old World 3rd Street, with its brick paving and German architecture. Spencer took her hand as they walked, and she didn't pull away. It seemed almost natural. A few blocks away they hit Wisconsin Avenue and the Grand Avenue Mall.

"Come on," Spencer said, pulling her across the street. "Häagen-Dazs is calling."

"Ice cream after that huge lunch?"

"Don't wimp out on me now, Georgia. Surely your appetite can handle a little rum raisin."

"Nope. It'll have to be something with chocolate. Otherwise, what's the point?"

They took the escalator to the third-floor Speisegarten, rising above the noise of the fountain below, the shoppers scurrying to and fro.

Sugar cones in hand, they took a table near the windows, looking out on the city streets below.

"I love how they put this mall together. They kept the old buildings intact, didn't mar any of their character or ruin the look of the city street."

"Is it how you would have designed it?"

"Pretty much. Well, maybe I would have used a little more glass."

"Where?" Georgia gasped. "The place is like a greenhouse."

"I like the limitless boundaries glass creates. The feeling of freedom."

"But that's just it, Spencer. It's only a feeling—an illusion. There's still a boundary. Try butting your heat against it and it may as well be a brick wall."

He leaned forward. "But you can see through it. You know what's on the other side. And you can break through it, if you really want to."

"Sure—and cut yourself up in the process."

"Life's full of injuries, Georgia. You can't always play it safe."

Yes, you can, she thought. The problem was, people around you didn't play it safe, and their fallout landed on you, changing your nice, safe course.

"Are you going to eat that ice cream or just let it melt all over your hand?"

Georgia looked down. "Oh, Lord—" She started lapping at the mess.

Elbow on the table, head in hand, Spencer settled in to watch the show. Her tongue flicked in and out, around and over, back and forth. "Ms. Moon, you're turning me on."

Georgia stopped midlick, peering at him over the mound of chocolate almond. "Then you're easy, Mr. Foxworth."

Spencer shook his head. "No, it's you, Georgia. These last few days, I've seen another side of you emerge. I always thought you were an attractive lady, but—"

"You thought I was attractive?" Georgia asked, a little stunned at the admission.

"Oh, yeah. Right from the start. Have you forgotten that pass I made all those years ago?"

Georgia shook her head. "No. I guess I just thought you made passes at all women."

Spencer laughed. "I'm not the womanizer you think I am, Georgia. Most of the women I've gotten involved with haven't wanted commitment any more than I have. Despite what you might think, there isn't a trail of broken hearts in my wake."

"Just a trail of very satisfied women, I suppose."

"I like to think so."

Georgia looked at the twinkle in his eye, the crooked grin on his lips. She could believe it. The man had Satisfaction Guaranteed written all over him.

He stood up abruptly and took her hand, pulling her out of her chair. "Come on."

Her mind still on satisfaction, Georgia felt a hot rush along her skin, her imagination reeling at the thought of where he might be hauling her off to. She dumped her unfinished cone in a garbage bin along the way to the escalator. He held her to his side, hand firmly at her waist, all the way down.

"Where are we going?" she asked a little breathlessly.

"We passed a pushcart on the way in. I saw something I want you to have."

"Oh." Was she disappointed? What had she wanted, to be hauled to the parking ramp and ravished amid the concrete pillars and engine fumes? Another satisfied customer?

Spencer pulled her over to a cart selling hats. Wonderful, wide-brimmed summer hats.

"That one." He pointed to a white hat with a black-and-white polka-dot scarf tied around its crown and steaming down its back.

"But, Spencer, I don't wear hats."

"The old Georgia didn't. The new, improved version does." He put it on her head. "Adorable." He kissed her on the nose. "Cute enough to belong to a woman named George."

She started to get mad, but didn't really feel like it. Instead, she checked out her reflection in a shop window. It did look pretty cute. She waited for Spencer to pay for it, then they walked through the mall, strolling hand in hand, stopping to window-shop, stopping to dig through sale bins and book racks.

Out on the street again, Georgia had to hold the hat to her head against a sudden gust of wind. She was laughing when she looked up at him. "You surprise me. I thought all men hated to shop."

"I'm no ordinary man. I keep trying to tell you that."

And she was starting to believe it. They stared at each other through an entire Walk light, almost getting run over by a bus when they didn't notice it had changed.

Once safely on the other side of the street, Spencer pulled her to a stop, swinging her into his arms. His gaze roamed over her face, shaded by the brim of her hat, her lips smiling, sun-kissed. "What would you do," he asked, "if I kissed you right here in the middle of the avenue?"

"I thought you believed in taking chances, Mr. Foxworth."

God, she could be cute when she teased him like this. Cute and sexy and fun. She had always been attractive, intelligent, stimulating. Today she was like no other woman. He wanted her more than he thought possible.

For a moment she thought he wasn't going to chance it. And she wanted him to. Wanted it with a fierce kind of longing she'd never known. Wanted to be kissed right here in the middle of the traffic and the people, the honking and the shouting. Wanted to be kissed by the best-looking, most charming man in the world. Wanted the world to see it. Wanted to be on the other side for a change, not watching, but doing.

And then his lips found hers and the rest of the world went away.

He kissed her thoroughly, leisurely. When he was finished, he took her face in his hands and looked at her like he couldn't get enough.

"I don't want this day to end—not yet. Come back home with me. We'll go for a swim, have dinner on the beach."

Lord, she was tempted. "Well, I do have to pick my car up—"

"Then say yes."

She looked into his eyes. "Yes. But, let's swing by my house so I can pick up my suit."

"Whatever you say." He kissed her again, quick and hard, and they practically ran all the way to the parking lot.

THEY PULLED UP in front of Georgia's house just as Emily was coming out, her arms piled with boxes. Georgia sat perfectly still while her daughter crammed more stuff into an already overloaded trunk. She watched without saying a word as Emily ran back to the house for more.

"Wait here," she told Spencer, afraid to even look at him.

"But, Georgia—"

She turned to him. "Just wait, okay? I need to talk to Emily and I don't need an audience—especially you."

He grabbed her arm as she started to get out of the car. "What's that supposed to mean?"

She threw him a look over her shoulder. "You're not stupid, Spencer. Figure it out."

She slammed the car door behind her and raced up the walk and into the house. Emily was just coming down the staircase, suitcase in hand.

"What's going on?"

"I'm taking my stuff over to the gallery."

"So soon?"

"Mom," Emily began with a long-suffering air, "I told you I'm renting a studio over there. You knew I was moving out."

"I know—I just didn't think it'd be so soon."

"Well, neither did I, but Spencer sent a check over today so—"

Georgia stopped listening. Lord, what a fool she was! All afternoon she'd been skipping though a romantic fantasy while Spencer probably knew exactly what Emily was up to. After all, he was the one financing it.

But why the kisses? Why the tender moments? Why the hat? She reached up and pulled it off, looking at it with disgust. Just what was Spencer up to? Did he want them both? Did he plan on two-timing the mother with the daughter and vice versa? Could he be that big a rat?

"Hah!" she said aloud. Of course he could be that big a rat. He was Spencer Foxworth, wasn't he? Not the womanizer she thought he was, indeed. No—he was worse. Much worse.

Emily was watching her strangely. "Mother, what is the matter with you?"

"Emily, I've got to tell you something. You've got to listen to me." She was done playing games. It was time for the direct approach. "Spencer is out in front of the house this very minute, waiting for me." She took a deep breath. "Emily, I've been with him all afternoon."

"Is he? Great. Now I can thank him in person."

Georgia grabbed her arm as she started for the door. "Did you hear me, Emily? We've been together all afternoon!"

"Mom, I think the heat has gotten to you." Emily patted Georgia's arm like she was some kind of raving mental invalid. "Of course you've been together all afternoon. You work for the man."

Georgia stared at her as she bounced out the door and down the steps. Spencer was leaning on the Jag, and she flew straight into his arms, giving him a big kiss on the cheek.

The arrogance of youth, Georgia thought. Emily couldn't possibly grasp that her own mother could be a rival.

Probably because she wasn't. Spencer was using her, keeping her away from the house while Emily moved out. He was flirting with her shamelessly, simply because for once she was receptive, and to him, flirting was like breathing.

Her mind scanned the afternoon. What an idiot she was! What a naive, daydreaming fool. How could she have almost fallen for it? Almost? She *had* fallen for it—hook, line and sinker. She'd been caught in the trap she'd baited herself.

Emily came running back into the house. "One more load and I'll be on my way—"

Georgia watched her run up the stairs, then she marched out of the house toward Spencer Foxworth.

He lounged against the hood of the Jag, muscular forearms crossed, hair lifting in the breeze. When he spotted her, he uncrossed his arms and came toward her, grinning.

"Emily sure is happy."

"As I'm sure you are, too," she replied stiffly.

His eyes squinted in puzzlement. "Well, sure. I mean it's been a great day." He put out a hand to touch her, running a finger down her nose and across her lips. "And it's going to be an even better night," he murmured.

She jerked away from his touch. "You've got to be joking."

Spencer put his hands in his pockets and sighed. "Georgia, what's the matter?"

"Don't ask me to talk about it now. Not after—" Not after I kissed you back and meant it, she finished in her mind. Not after that damned well-practiced charm of yours made me forget my whole reason for being with you. "Just leave, Spencer. Please." She turned from him and started for the house.

He grabbed her arm, whirling her around to face him. "But what about dinner? What about our swim?"

"You can't be serious? How can you think I'd go through with that after—" she looked at the house, her arm lifting and falling. Somehow she couldn't say the words out loud. "After—after this—"

"Look, you have to pick up your car, anyway. Let's go for a drive. Talk this out."

"I'm not going anywhere with you. I'll take a cab to work tomorrow."

"Georgia, sweetheart, I understand that you're upset about Emily. But she's a big girl now. It's time for you to let go—time for you to start living your own life—and let Emily live hers."

She twisted her arm out of his grasp. "How dare you!"

His eyes narrowed, darkening with anger. "*How dare I? What* is this, Georgia? I'm okay for an afternoon's distraction, okay for a few kisses, a few laughs, but I better stay out of your personal life? Is that it?"

"That's it, Spencer. Stay out of my personal life— and stay away from my daughter!"

Chapter Eight

Spencer was finding it hard to concentrate on the design for the Hawkinses' kitchen. He kept sneaking looks at Georgia just to make sure she was really there, in his kitchen, cooking something that smelled wonderful. After yesterday he'd wondered if she'd even show up for work today. But here she was, making him lunch, humming softly while she moved about his house.

And he loved the sight of it. He loved the idea of it. He loved the smell of it—chicken sautéing, something spicy simmering. What was happening to his freedom-loving soul? The idea of Georgia Moon making herself at home in his kitchen was more arousing than her lying on his beach in a skimpy swimsuit.

Well, maybe not. Spencer grinned to himself. Georgia in a skimpy anything was a pretty good idea, too.

And that reminded him of the swim they never took, of the dinner they never shared. How had all that anger of the day before turned into chicken and spice? He had a very firm suspicion that the woman was up to more than making him lunch. He just wasn't sure what.

Georgia rummaged in Spencer's glass-front refrigerator, looking for soy sauce. Actually, what she'd like to find was a little liquid arsenic, or maybe some hemlock root. The swine deserved to die, and here she was preparing to feed him. It'd serve him right if it was the last meal he ever ate.

She glanced up to find him looking at her. She forced a smile, sweet and sexy. She'd almost blown all the progress she'd made yesterday when she'd come home to find Emily moving out with the help of Spencer's nice, fat check in her pocket. It was costing her all her self-control to put the sight of Emily rushing down the stairs and into his arms out of her mind.

But maybe she shouldn't try to forget. Maybe that was exactly the image she needed to keep herself from ever coming close to forgetting her mission again. Because yesterday afternoon she'd almost done just that. She'd almost forgotten that she was with Spencer only for Emily's sake. Almost. And then she'd almost blown it by telling him off, by telling him to stay away from Emily. She figured she better make up for it fast. Her Singapore chicken salad with snow peas was a start.

Spencer's kitchen was done in a gleaming Euro-style—very techno, very modern. White on white, with only a smattering of bright blue and a sort of sandy color for relief. Georgia had hated it on sight, telling herself she preferred ruffled curtains at the window and the homey warmth of bright yellow wallpaper. But having just cooked for the first time in Spencer's gleaming wonder, Georgia had to admit that it was the most efficiently designed kitchen she'd ever puttered in.

"You know what they say about the way to a man's heart, don't you, Georgia?"

Georgia's head jerked up. She hadn't heard him move, but there he was, halfway across the room, sprawled on the buff-colored leather sectional, watching her.

"Shouldn't you be working instead of lying around, spouting clichés?"

Spencer chuckled. "I'm finding the idea of a beautiful woman puttering in my kitchen fascinating."

Georgia snorted. "Now you sound like a male chauvinist pig."

"To prove I'm not, I'll do the dishes."

Georgia stared at him. His loose, thin cotton trousers draped over his body, outlining the well-defined muscles in his thighs. His simple, expensive, white cotton shirt was rolled at the sleeves, open at the throat. His skin was tan, taut. His grin was appealing, slightly naughty. Georgia figured there should be a law against looking the way he did.

"Come over here, Georgia."

His voice floated down her spine, sending weakness in its wake. "I'm busy," she answered briskly.

"That's what I'm wondering about. Why are you so busy? What's with the domestic bit?"

"I thought you liked seeing a woman puttering in your kitchen."

"Oh, I do. But last night you were furious with me and now you're cooking me lunch. What are you up to?"

"I'm up to the part where you add the mayonnaise."

Spencer stood and started toward her. "You know that's not what I meant. Why all the sweetness and light this morning when you were so mad at me last night?"

"I—I—" He was standing behind her now, leaning in close enough for her to smell the scent of his cologne. It smelled like the wind and the waves, like freedom and blue sky. He braced one hand on the counter next to her and reached around with the other to pluck a snow pea from the bowl she was stirring. She could hear the soft sound of his chewing in her ear.

"You what?" he murmured.

"I just wanted to make amends for acting so bitchy last night. You were only trying to help and—"

"And you're lying."

Georgia spun around. A mistake. He was only inches from her. "What do you mean? Why would I lie?"

His navy gaze scanned her face. "I don't know. But you're up to something." His eyes narrowed. "Or maybe you're after something? Yeah—" he leaned in closer, placing his other hand on the counter "—I think that's it. You're using feminine wiles to get something." His eyes focused on her mouth. "I just wish I knew what it was," he murmured. He shifted his gaze to her startled eyes, resting his body lightly against hers. "Or how far you'd be willing to go to get it."

Georgia's mouth dropped open in a gasp. "I'm sure I don't know what you're talking about. I'm— I'm—" How was she supposed to think with his body pressing against hers? How was she supposed to concentrate on saying the right thing, on not giving the game away? And now what was he doing? Nuzzling her neck. Oh, Lord.

She closed her eyes for the briefest of seconds, allowing herself one tiny moment of thrill, one little second of hot blood rushing through her veins.

"Spencer?"

"Hmm," he murmured against her neck.

"Aren't you hungry?" she asked lamely.

He laughed softly. "Starving, sweetheart." His lips moved up her throat to nibble on her chin. "This is a hell of an appetizer. I can't wait for the main course."

Georgia reached desperately behind her and grabbed the salad bowl. "Here." She thrust it at him. "Singapore chicken salad."

Spencer stopped nibbling in time to grab the bowl before it went crashing to the floor. He looked down at it. "Not exactly what I had in mind, but it looks delicious."

"Why don't you take it out on the patio and I'll get the dishes."

"Okay." He gave her a meaningful leer. "Don't be too long."

"DELICIOUS," Spencer said, putting down his fork and taking a sip of iced tea. He looked at her speculatively over the rim of his glass. The sun was on her hair, the breeze blowing strands across her face. She wore something gauzy today—a midcalf skirt and a peasant blouse that kept slipping off one smooth, white shoulder.

He wanted her. But, even more, he wanted to know why the sudden change in her. She was thawing toward him, but she was definitely nervous about it. He'd be willing to bet she was as affected as he whenever he got close, but she was just a little bit scared of it. "Things all set for tomorrow night?"

"All set."

"The extremely efficient Ms. Moon. I'm sure the party will be a great success." Leaning forward, he picked up her hand, holding it lightly. "I'm looking forward to the evening, George. I'm looking forward to having you on my arm."

Georgia swallowed hard as he raised her hand to his mouth, pressing his lips into her palm. She wanted to snatch her hand away, but he was already suspicious. She couldn't keep running hot and cold on him or he would guess what she was up to. Emily would end up in his clutches and there would be nothing she could do about it.

But right now, it was her hand in his clutches. And he seemed in no hurry to let go.

"Maybe you can stay for dinner after the party. Or " He pressed his lips to her palm again.

"Or?" she croaked.

"Or a moonlight swim. Better bring your suit along, just in case."

"Sure." She meant to say it casually, as if moonlight swims with sexy, gorgeous, potent playboys were an everyday occurrence for her, but the word stuck in her throat, making her sound more like a nervous virgin.

She watched him warily as he stood up, still holding her hand, and moved to her side of the table. He drew her up and into his arms.

"Wha—what are you doing?"

"I'm thanking you for that delicious lunch, George."

His mouth covered hers, his arms pressed her close. Heat sprang up through the length of her body, intensifying along her back where he moved his hands and melting her knees so she had to cling to him or risk puddling at his feet.

His mouth moved expertly, touching lightly, deepening smoothly. His tongue feathered its way inside, playing with hers until she could no longer hold back, until she matched his moves eagerly. Her body was on fire, alive, pulsing with energy. She started to touch him.

Spencer had meant the kiss to unsettle her, to tease her, to see how far she'd go. But it knocked him reeling. The first tentative touches of her tongue set his pulse racing. Her hands lightly moving over his shoulders, her fingers delving shyly into his hair, her soft, untutored moan, made him more needy, hotter than any forays by practiced, experienced women had ever done.

He broke the kiss, tearing his mouth from hers, breathing hard against her skin. "George, George—I don't know what you're up to, but do you know what you're doing to me?" He pulled back and looked into her face. He was doing the same to her, he'd stake his life on it. "Sweetheart," he murmured. And then he was kissing her again.

And she forgot all about Emily.

He sat in a patio chair and pulled her onto his lap. He ran his hands through her wind-tangled hair. He watched the sun play across her face. He kissed her, over and over again.

And she kissed him back.

Cupping her face, he looked into her amber eyes. "I used to dream about you, you know that? I'd wake up in the morning wanting you, waiting for you. Then you'd walk in the door, efficient, brisk, all business. It used to drive me crazy."

She shook her head. "I don't believe you." But she wanted to. Oh, she wanted to.

"It's true." He kissed her nose, her eyes. "Didn't you ever dream about me?"

She shook her head, but the blush on her cheeks told him differently.

"You did, didn't you?"

"Of course not," she said primly, but then she buried her face in his chest.

"God, you're sweet. You know that, George?" He stroked her sun-warmed hair, loving the feel of her in his arms. He'd set out to torment her, to maybe find out what game she was playing, but it had all turned real so quickly, so easily. He put a finger under her chin, bringing her face up to his.

"Let's take the afternoon off. We'll drive out to the Hawkins site, walk through the plans together. I'd love for you to see it. We can stop for dinner out in the country somewhere—"

Behind them, in the house, the phone rang. Georgia started to wiggle out of his arms.

"No—don't answer it. Let the machine get it."

Eloise Hawkins's shrill voice split the air. "Spencer, honey, where the hell are you? You said you'd be here about one, sugar. Now, do I have to come over there and find you? You get those cute buns of yours over here!"

Spencer groaned. "For a woman who undoubtedly needs a recipe to make toast, she's certainly eager to see those kitchen plans."

Georgia started to pull out of his lap. "It's you she's eager to see."

Spencer caught her by the waist, stopping her, his voice almost fierce. "It's not mutual. You know that, don't you, George?"

She pushed his hands away and stood up. "That's really none of my business, is it?"

He was on his feet in an instant, pulling her back into his arms. "Like hell it isn't." His mouth covered hers again, hard, demanding. She struggled, but only for a moment, and then her arms were around him, and she matched him, heat for heat. It was savage, it was lusty and it seemed right. So very right.

The phone started to ring again and Spencer pulled away, his breath coming hard. He stared at her, brushing his thumb across her lips. "You're driving me crazy, George," he whispered, fighting for breath. "One minute you're—" he moved his head impatiently "—and the next—"

She pulled away just as Eloise's voice split the air again.

"You'd better go, Spencer. She's expecting you."

"I don't want to go. I want to stay here with you. We need to talk, George...."

Talk was the last thing she needed. Well, maybe not the very last. The very last thing she needed was for him to touch her again, to kiss her again. She was so confused—so hot. She lifted the hair off the back of her neck, but the movement of her breasts against the soft gauze of her blouse only reminded her of how much she ached to be touched. She had to get away from him. She headed for the patio doors.

"No, Spencer. Go. You made the appointment, now keep it. And stop calling me George!"

SPENCER WAS HALFWAY to Eloise's when he pulled the Jag into a U-turn and headed back to the house. How was he supposed to concentrate when all he could do was think of how she felt in his arms, the taste of her mouth, the sound of her sigh? How could a grown woman be so innocently arousing, so maddeningly contradictory? He'd meant to teach her a lesson that afternoon, to push her so far that she'd finally confess what she was up to. Instead, the tables had been turned. Once again, Ms. Georgia Moon had wound him up tight and let him crash and burn.

Eloise could damn well wait. He was going back to settle this thing with George, once and for all. Either they'd spend the rest of the afternoon fighting, or they'd spend it making love. He fervently hoped it would be the latter.

He was in such a state when he pulled into his drive that he didn't even notice her car was gone. It wasn't until he'd stormed in the house, calling her name, that he realized she'd already left.

FRIDAY, GEORGIA ARRIVED at work carrying her new dress in its plastic bag, and a small overnight case. Despite the fact that showering and dressing in Spencer's bathroom seemed a little dangerous, she told herself it was pointless to drive all the way home to change, then rush back for the party. In any case, there was little reason to go home these days. Jasmine was absorbed in her paints and canvas, and Emily was ensconced in her new studio, hopefully spending her evenings with a welding mask and torch. Despite the fact that Georgia had been alone a good portion of her forty years, she was beginning to feel lonely, in need of companionship. She was beginning to feel a lot of things.

She hung the dress in the little powder room under the stairs. When she turned around, Spencer was there.

His expression was grim. "What the hell happened to you yesterday?" he demanded.

"What do you mean?" she asked, her feigned nonchalance spoiled by a sudden catch in her voice.

"What do I mean?" He took a step forward, blocking her way, holding her in the doorway. "I decided not to go to Eloise's, but by the time I rushed back here, you were already gone."

"Well, I had stuff to do—errands and things—for tonight. You never objected to me leaving early before."

"I never had you in my arms before."

Georgia's breath caught in her throat. His voice seemed to have been excavated from deep in his chest for the sole purpose of sending a chill down her spine. His eyes, the deepest blue she'd ever seen this side of a china doll, were too hot to be playful, too intent to be ignored. Georgia gulped.

"Is that your dress for tonight?" he asked, his eyes flickering to the garment hanging in the room behind her.

"Yes. . . ."

"Do I get to see it?" he asked.

She shook her head. "No, it's a surprise."

His gaze moved back to her, his smile coming slowly. "You're the surprise," he said, and then he reached for her.

"Now, Spencer," Georgia scolded, her heart beating in panic as she slapped his hands away. "I don't think we should start fooling around at work again."

"I'd be glad to fool around with you anywhere you say, if I could only find you." His expression turned grim again, his eyes narrowed. "Where the hell were you last night? I called and called—even drove over. The house was dark and closed up."

Georgia was very aware of that. She'd been hiding in her bedroom with the phone unplugged, reading a book by flashlight. It had been one of those lewdly covered romances that, under the circumstances, she had no business reading.

"Well?" he demanded.

"Well what?" Georgia stammered, hoping she hadn't missed anything important.

Spencer sighed and put his hands on the doorframe on either side of her. "Where were you last night?" He shifted his body, settling it more heavily in her direction. "After what happened on the patio yesterday, you must have known I'd want to see you, to talk things out."

His voice had deepened, slowed. Too bad it didn't have that effect on her heart. Her limbs felt liquid, but her throat went dry as she croaked out, "I—I told you—I had a lot to do for the party...."

One hand came away from the doorframe, his fingers untangling strands of hair that had caught on her eyelashes, smoothing them out, settling them gently into the rest of her hair. When his eyes came back to hers, they looked amused. "With all these preparations, I can only assume, Ms. Moon, that this is going to be one hell of a party." His fingers still in her hair, his thumb started to work her earlobe, back and forth lightly. "Do you know what part I'm looking forward to?"

"Mmm?" she got out. She didn't have the breath to say more.

"Afterward, when everyone's left and we're alone. Because that's when we—you and I, Ms. Moon—are going to have a little talk." His fingers trailed down the line of her jaw to cup her chin. That playful thumb brushed her lips this time and Georgia stopped breathing altogether, her lips parting in anticipation, her body leaning forward yearningly with a will of its own. Spencer dropped his hand and stepped back. "Tonight, Ms. Moon—you can count on it." Then he gave her a quick kiss on the forehead and walked away.

SPENCER WAS OUT all day. By necessity or design, Georgia didn't care, just as long as she didn't have to deal with him—or her body's traitorous reactions. She passed the day making final preparations for the party, steadfastly refusing to think of what she had gotten herself into, or what might happen after this little talk he seemed intent on having.

Just after four, Spencer breezed in, his tux, swathed in plastic from the cleaners, thrown over his shoulder, a box from the florist tucked under his arm.

"Everything all set?"

"All set. The caterers should be here by five, the guests by six. I just have to take my shower and change."

"The place looks great, Georgia. The flowers are beautiful."

Georgia beamed. "Thanks. I arranged them myself."

Spencer looked at her in surprise. "Really? I certainly didn't expect you to do that, sweetheart."

Georgia shrugged. "It's cheaper. Besides they look nicer—softer, not so stiff and formal."

"You look a little tired. Here—" he took the last floral arrangement from her and set it on the coffee table, then took her hand and led her to the sofa "—you sit. I'll get you a glass of wine."

"I should still—"

He pressed her back to the sofa by the shoulders. "There can't be anything left to do, sweetheart. If there is, just let me know and I'll do it."

She *was* a little tired. She watched him go to the kitchen area and pour her a glass of wine. He came back and handed it to her. "Enjoy," he said. Then he bent and brushed her lips with his. "I'll go take my shower first while you relax. Then I'll deal with the caterers while you get ready."

Before she could protest, he was gone, up the stairs. Minutes later she heard the shower going.

She sipped the cool, crisp wine, feeling it flow through her, letting it relax her. The sound of waves ebbed in through the open patio doors. She watched the gulls swooping, watched a sailboat in the distance. For the first time, the house struck her as peaceful, its sparse, modern lines and uncluttered furnishings blending with the lull of the waves and the freedom of the gulls.

The colors and textures Spencer had chosen for his house without walls blended with the color of the lake and the sky and the sand at the water's edge. Just as the Murdoch house blended with its setting.

He was a talented man, a sensitive man.

And tonight he could be hers. The beat of her heart at the fantasy had nothing to do with saving Emily, and everything to do with herself. True, if she let herself have him, just for this one night, she could tell Emily. It would be over, and her daughter would be out of Spencer's reach forever.

Was she prepared to go that far? And if she did, would it be for Emily—or would it be for herself?

She heard the water stop, heard him come out of the bathroom. She drained her wineglass, closing her eyes for a moment. She was tired of thinking, tired of trying to sort it all out. Maybe for the next few hours she could give herself the gift of enjoying the present, a small oasis of time where she wouldn't have to think—she'd only have to do and feel.

Yes. They wouldn't be alone for hours. She could afford to take the time. She could afford to enjoy the party.

Carrying her dress and case, she made her way upstairs, expecting to find Spencer dressed. But he wasn't.

He stood at the open balcony doors, his back to the room, naked but for a terry towel draped around his lean hips.

"Oh, I'm sorry. I thought—" Georgia stammered.

He turned around. The blue of the towel matched his eyes. But that wasn't all Georgia noticed. He was all tan, lean muscle. The hair on his chest was damp and curled, beads of water clinging to the dark whorls. The hair on his head was wet, slicked back, accentuating the carved planes of his face. The man was gorgeous—dangerously so. How could she think she could lure him away from any woman? How could she think she could make him want her, even for one night?

Her eyes traveled lower, and to her astonishment she could see that he did indeed want her—and now. Clutching her dress to her bosom, Georgia started to back away. "I'm sorry, I thought— I'll—I'll wait downstairs until you're finished." She winced at her choice of words, her eyes darting again to the towel and what it covered. "I mean, until you're dressed," she finished lamely.

Spencer laughed softly. "Come over here, Georgia."

She shook her head, but her feet inexplicably moved forward. She couldn't seem to make them stop. He met her halfway, coming close enough for her to smell the fresh dampness of his skin.

He took the dress from her, tearing off the plastic cover with one deft swipe of his hand. He looked at it, then at her.

"You're going to look beautiful in this, Georgia. I can't wait to see you." He handed the dress back to her. "Go get ready," he said. "The bathroom's all yours."

Clutching the dress, she made a hasty retreat, feeling like a criminal who'd just gotten a reprieve. Just before she shut the bathroom door, he spoke.

"Georgia?"

"Yes?" she answered, her legs turning to jelly.

"You better lock the door," he said. And she did.

Chapter Nine

She stood naked in Spencer's bathroom, the steam from his shower still moist in the air. The scent of his warmed cologne caressed her, heightening Georgia's senses. There was something magical at work; she knew it in the way the new dress floated over her body as she slipped it on, settling against her skin like it'd been created just for her. She knew it in the slight, bright wave of her hair, the blush on her cheeks, the fullness of her lips. She felt beautiful. She felt alive.

She descended the stairs, and he was there below her, watching, waiting, looking breathtakingly handsome and completely at home in his dark tux and crisp white shirt.

Spencer watched the dress swirling about her long, shapely legs, watched her hips swaying slightly, her breasts moving lightly. She was a sight; she was his Georgia. And she *was* going to be his.

Whatever game she was playing, it was ending tonight. What was between them was real. After tonight, she would no longer be able to deny it, either.

"You look even lovelier than I could have imagined," he murmured when she reached him. He took her hand and raised it to his lips.

The feel of his mouth brushing over her knuckles, and the look in his dark, sparkling eyes, sent her heart soaring. She had never felt more beautiful, more alive.

"This is for you." He held out a creamy white gardenia to her. She took it in her fingers, the heady, exotic scent floating around her.

"It's beautiful. Thank you." She looked down at her dress, but there didn't seem to be enough material to pin it to.

"Your hair, I think," he murmured, taking the flower from her and fastening it above her ear.

His touch was so tender, so intimate, as he smoothed the hair behind her ear, all she could do was stare and hope that he couldn't see her heart beating through her dress.

The sound of the doorbell broke the spell and Georgia took a breath of relief.

"Come, let's greet our guests," Spencer said, offering his arm, tucking her in close to his side.

Our guests. Not *my* guests. With a few words, a simple gesture, he made them into a couple.

And that's how everyone viewed them—these men, elegant in their tuxedos, these women, with that special patina of grace and style that only the wealthy or creative seemed to attain.

Georgia was easily swept into their circle. Some of the men she had already met, but none of them treated her like Spencer's assistant, a paid hostess for the event. Instead, she was treated like Spencer's woman, and she didn't in the least feel like correcting this mistaken notion.

"Georgia, my dear, it's good to see you and Spencer together at last." This from Burke Cummings, a distinguished, handsome man with gray in his hair and a twinkle in his pale blue eyes. "I know how fond he has always been of you. It's good to see you together."

"Yes," concurred his wife, Adrienne, a willowy, tall creature with her white hair drawn tightly back from her elegantly boned face. "You were wise to let him sow his wild oats before getting involved, my dear. I must say the strategy seems to have worked—the man is obviously devoted to you."

"But—" Georgia began. She was saved, however, from replying to this erroneous bit of information by Spencer himself.

"Sweetheart," he murmured, coming up behind her and placing a proprietary hand at her waist, "if the Cummingses will let me steal you away, there's someone I want you to meet."

With Burke and Adrienne's smiling approval, Spencer steered her toward another couple.

"Georgia, I'd like you to meet Harry Matthews and his wife, Bonnie."

"Ah—" Harry took her hand and brought it close to his lips "—the voice on the phone." His grin close to a leer, he looked her over from head to toe. "I'm gratified to see that you look every bit as sexy as you sound."

Bonnie elbowed him. "For heaven's sake, Harry, behave yourself." She turned to Georgia. "Honestly, a couple of glasses of wine and I can't take him anywhere."

Georgia laughed. "I've spoken to Mr. Matthews many times on the phone. It's a pleasure to meet him finally, face-to-face."

"Call him Harry. He's already nearly impossible to live with since he won that award for the Oberman estate."

"Yes, I heard the project was spectacular. Congratulations, Harry."

Matthews beamed and seemed about to say something, but Bonnie cut him off.

"Don't encourage him, Georgia. He's full of himself enough already. I'm Bonnie." She held out her hand. "We've been looking forward to meeting you. Spencer has spoken so often of you over the years, we almost feel we know you."

And this was how the entire evening went. No one seemed surprised to see her there in the capacity of hostess, or in the capacity of Spencer's woman. Georgia warmed to the tone of the evening with surprising ease, taking Spencer's hand to lead him over to a new arrival, putting their heads together to discuss the state of the wine supply, accepting his quick, light kiss when he praised her for the success of the food.

Outside, the late May sky turned to rose, bathing the room with an ethereal light, adding to the enchantment. Across the room, Spencer caught her eye. His smile was intimate, warm. It sent a thrill of promise through her, and she glanced at the clock, suddenly eager for the guests to leave.

AT LAST THEY STOOD, hand in hand in the open doorway, waving to the final departures. They turned to each other, crazy grins on their faces.

"So," Spencer said.

"So," echoed Georgia.

A metallic crash came from the kitchen area, and Spencer groaned. "How long do you think they'll take to clean up?"

"Not long. I'll go help them."

But Spencer wouldn't let go of her hand. "I'm afraid that if I don't keep touching you, some spell will be broken, and you'll run out of here leaving only your shoe behind for me to hold on to."

"I'm not going anywhere," she told him, surprised that her voice sounded so steady.

He started to lower his head to hers.

"Excuse me." One of the caterers stood with arms loaded, trying to get through the doorway Spencer and Georgia were blocking.

They looked at each other and, laughing, moved out of the way. Georgia gave Spencer a little shove toward the sectional, telling him to sit, before going to help with the last of the cleanup. When the caterers finally left, she came and stood before him.

He held out his hand to her. "Sit with me and share the sunset."

She took his hand and slid in next to him. His other arm went around her and she leaned her head on his shoulder. They watched the darkening sky in silence.

After a while, Spencer let out a deep sigh. He kissed her hair and tucked her head under his chin. "I can't believe you're here like this with me. I can't believe you're letting me hold you, kiss you. It's like a dream."

His words troubled her, sending a stab of fear and guilt. She pulled away a little to look into his face.

"Am I scaring you? Moving too fast?" His hand went to her face, his palm caressing her cheek, his fingers pushing into her hair. "I can't help it, Georgia. I want you too much to pretend."

Pretend. She looked into his eyes. Tell him now, she thought, before this goes any further. Tell him what you've been up to. Tell him it's all been a game.

But then she would have to leave and she would never have this again—this feeling of being wanted, this feeling of being beautiful, feminine, desired. She wanted to hold on to the magic the night had given her, hold it in her heart and feel it course through her veins. She wanted the magic. She wanted him. Just this once.

She put her hand over his, holding his caress to her face, leaning into his touch. "I want you, too," she said.

The tension in Spencer melted at her words. He closed his eyes, letting out his breath, pulling her into him, holding her—just holding her. For tonight, she was his. Tomorrow could take care of itself.

When he kissed her, it was with a tenderness that he hadn't known he possessed. He was prepared to take all the time in the world in this final wooing of Ms. Georgia Moon.

Tentatively, he began to stroke her, heating her pulse, feeling her blood as it started to pound. He caressed her bare shoulders, the skin silky as a dream. His hands ran down her sides, skimming the outer flow of her full breasts. She moaned, moving restlessly in his arms, arching toward his touch.

When his hand gently covered her breast, he felt the jolt go through her. She was hungry, starved, and it sent him over the edge.

Tearing his mouth from hers, he forgot about patience. His fingers edged beneath the thin straps of her dress, pulling them off her shoulders, covering the newly bared flesh with openmouthed kisses.

She didn't stop him. She wanted this. God, how she wanted it. She shoved her fingers into his hair, holding his mouth against her flesh, gasping at the feelings tearing through her body. He brought his head up to claim her mouth again and she met his urgency with a fierceness of her own. He pushed his hand down her dress, capturing her nipple between his fingers, and with his mouth still covering hers, she cried out.

"Georgia, my God," he whispered against her skin, raining kisses down her neck and shoulders, biting her throbbing flesh through the fabric of her dress. His hand ran up her leg, under her dress, touching the bare flesh above the top of her stocking.

Suddenly he pulled away from her, grinning down at her where she lay in breathless disarray. "You're wearing a garter belt, aren't you?"

Her eyes widened as she tried to catch her breath. "What?" she asked between pants.

"What else have you got on under there?" he asked, running his hands over her, covering her breasts with his palms. Abruptly, he stood up. "Come on," he said, taking her hand.

"You're stopping?" she gasped.

He smiled down at her. "Sweetheart, we're just getting started." He pulled her to her feet, holding on to her when it seemed her legs might not hold her. "Look at me, Georgia."

When her head came languidly up, it was all he could do to keep from pulling her back to the sofa and finishing what he started. Her eyes were clouded with passion, her skin flushed with it. But he wanted more than just a tumble on the sofa with this woman. He wanted her in his bed where he could hold her all night, love her all night. But first he wanted to see what was under that dress.

"We're not kids, Georgia. I don't want to take you, half-dressed, on the living room sofa like we're doing something rushed, something wrong. Come upstairs with me."

Not trusting herself to speak, she nodded mutely, allowing herself to be led by the hand as they climbed the stairs.

The night had nearly closed the sky and the bedroom was dim. Spencer flicked a switch and a small lamp came on, illuminating the huge bed covered in beige silk with a rosy glow. He flipped another switch and the ceiling fan began to whir softly, sending a faint, cool breeze through the air.

Georgia stared at him, entranced, as he started to undress, releasing his bow tie, tossing aside his jacket, unbuttoning his shirt. She gulped against her dry throat, wishing he had taken her on the sofa. It would be over by now and she wouldn't have to undress in front of him.

But it seemed she wouldn't have to, after all—at least, not by herself. Once he'd discarded his shirt, he walked slowly over to her, cupping the nape of her neck in his hands, his mouth grazing hers lightly, leaving her hungry for more. His hands moved over her shoulders, coming into contact with her dress, pulling it down over her body until it lay pooled at her feet.

The fan-stirred air felt delicious against her bare skin, almost making her forget to be shy. When she met his eyes, there was enough heat there to render the coldest air conditioner useless.

His eyes raked over the ivory lace bustier with its attached garters holding up her pale, sheer stockings, stopping to rest for a moment on the triangle of lace that barely covered her. "The prim Ms. Moon is just full of little surprises," he said, his mouth quirking into a sexy half grin.

"W-well," she stammered, "you can't wear just anything under a dress like that."

He laughed softly. "You're right, this certainly isn't just anything." He pulled her into his arms.

"Ms. Moon, discovering who you really are is giving me the greatest of pleasure."

Before she could say anything, he was kissing her, running his hands down her back, pulling her tight against him. Before she'd had nearly enough, he released her. Dropping to his knees, he peeled her stockings down her legs, running his tongue up the length of each thigh. She rocked on her feet and his arms went around her waist, holding her up, as his tongue traced the outline of the top of her panties and delved into her navel.

She shuddered. "Spencer—"

He looked up at her. "Want me to stop?"

She shook her head wildly. "No—oh, no. . . ."

His laughter rumbled softly against her stomach. "Okay, Ms. Moon, you're the boss." He grabbed the bit of silk and lace with his teeth, lowering it slowly, and she thought she'd die. The air seemed electrified against this newly exposed part of her body, and she quivered, meeting his eyes when he looked up at her. Their gazes seemed riveted for an instant, and she became afraid. Her lips parted, as if to speak, as if to tell him *No, stop, we can't*—and then his mouth covered her and she forgot to think. Her head snapped back and she cried out. Her fingers convulsed, digging into his shoulders, and then she just rode with it. Wave after wave of feeling slammed through her, building, centering, begging for release. Suddenly he let her go, standing to pull her into his arms. She heard ragged breathing. His? Her own? They seemed bound together as one heaving flesh.

His hands fumbled with the zipper of the bustier, and he peeled the ivory lace from her body and tossed it aside. And then he just looked at her.

Her body throbbed under his gaze, grieving for his touch, longing for something that her fevered mind could only guess existed.

"You're more beautiful than I dreamed," he said, his voice husky, foreign in his throat.

He swept her into his arms and carried her to the bed, laying her down on the cool, cool sheets. She watched him unzip his pants and let them drop. And then he joined her on the bed and began to make love to her.

GEORGIA STIRRED in her sleep, moving her cheek against Spencer's chest, her arm settling more heavily across his belly. Spencer, propped up against two pillows and wide awake, looked down at her.

He should have been exhausted and sleeping like a baby. But he didn't want to sleep. He couldn't get enough of touching her, of looking at her.

In bed, there was an innocence to her that belied the womanly curves of her body, the faint marks that forty years of living had left on her face. Innocently passionate. An uncertain volcano, exploding, erupting, and he had reveled in the molten heat of it, getting as much as he gave, learning as much as he had already known. Despite the many young women that had graced his life and his bed, Spencer knew now that he had never been with a real woman before. His body had been satisfied, but his heart had never been touched.

Georgia stirred again, rolling away from him onto her back. One knee was bent, crossed over her other leg. Her face was turned away from him and her arms were raised, one resting above her head, the other with its hand resting against her cheek, the fingers touching her slightly parted lips.

Her breasts were beautiful, full and rounded. Her hips flared out from the curve of her waist. Her legs—her legs were long, full, curving down to trim ankles. And her feet— Spencer chuckled softly. He'd never been moved by a woman's feet before.

But then, he'd never been moved by a woman before. She was a complex package, a mystery she hid from the world.

Lately, he had seen glimpses of the woman behind the wall. Tonight, in his arms, she had come out for a while—and she was glorious. And he wasn't going to let her go.

Spencer scooted down and gathered her into his arms. She sighed and stirred, but she didn't waken. Her arms glided easily around him, her body settling heavily against him. Spencer smiled and drifted off to sleep at last.

WHEN HE AWOKE, he was alone. The sky was beginning to lighten, leaving an unsettled, hazy darkness in the room. The space beside him was empty, but her dress still lay pooled on the floor. He got out of bed to find her.

Georgia stood on the balcony, the silk comforter from the bed wrapped around her, leaving her shoulders bare. Shivering slightly, she pulled the comforter closer, wondering why she was standing there listening to the waves, watching the sky race toward dawn. Why hadn't she left when she'd woken to find Spencer still asleep beside her?

Her mission was accomplished. She had succeeded in seducing Spencer, in ruining anything he might have had with Emily. Now all that remained was to tell her daughter where she'd been all night. So why was she still here? And why, instead of sweet triumph, did she feel only confusion?

Naked, Spencer stepped out onto the balcony behind her. "Why are you here with me now, after all these years?"

Georgia couldn't turn around and face him. It was a question she'd dreaded. She should have left while he was asleep; she should have grabbed her clothes and ran while she had the chance. Instead, she fought the question with one of her own.

"Why are *you* here with *me*?"

"Maybe because you're allowing it."

She did turn and face him then, trying to keep her voice light, ironic. "The quintessential playboy, taking whatever is offered?"

He shook his head and started toward her. "I'm no playboy, Georgia. You were always wrong about that. I've wanted my freedom, but so have the women I've been with. Mutual pleasure, mutual parting."

She turned away from him. "I couldn't live like that."

"I know that. I know, for a woman like you, it's different. And knowing that, I still made love to you last night."

Georgia stiffened, pulling the comforter more tightly around her. "What are you saying?"

"I'm saying that maybe freedom isn't so important anymore."

He was right behind her now; she could feel the heat from his sleep-warmed body against her bare shoulders. She closed her eyes and bit her lip, fighting the seduction of his closeness, the promise of his words. She didn't want him to say any more, but she seemed powerless to stop it.

"I'm saying," he murmured, sliding his arms around her and pulling her back against him, "that maybe I'm falling in love with you."

The words hurt her more than she could have dreamed. Could she believe him? And if she believed him, what had she done?

He nuzzled her neck, feeling a shiver go through her. "Say something, Georgia. Tell me how you feel."

She wiggled around to face him. "I don't know how I feel," she answered. And it was the truth, maybe the most honest words she'd ever uttered.

He gazed into her face for long moments, then the ghost of a grin touched his mouth. He tugged at the comforter. "Come on, open up and let me in. It's chilly out here."

She parted the silk and drew him in, pulling it around him. "Better?"

"Mmm, much."

His hands skimmed over her, and she caught her breath, lifting her face for his kiss. She started to ache in places that should have been numb after last night. She could want him so fast, so urgently, it was frightening. She should pull away from him, she knew, but the magic was nearly as strong at sunrise as it had been at sunset. But she shouldn't let it happen—not again. It didn't need to happen again—

"Ever make love to the sunrise?" he whispered.

"No," she answered breathlessly. There were so many things she'd never done.

"Come over here," he murmured, leading her to a padded chaise lounge. He pulled her down with him so that she was sprawled on top of him, the comforter still covering them.

"Here?" she gasped.

"Here and now, sweetheart," Spencer answered, his mouth moving over her neck and shoulders.

"But we're outside—someone might see."

"Just Mother Nature, sweetheart, and she won't care."

Georgia arched up to look around. Spencer took the opportunity to take her breast into his mouth. His tongue drove everything else from her mind. Reason exploded, scattering to the wind, and eagerly she reached for him.

Hands searched and captured, lips sought and found. The beige silk slithered and undulated over bodies dancing in passion. Whispers and sighs rode the predawn stillness, drowning in the waves on the beach below.

The sky grew lighter, and a lip of pure gold appeared on the horizon, melting the last of the night. Georgia rose up to straddle him, taking him into her heat, riding him into ecstasy, and the sun rose behind her, spilling blazing color across the sky.

Spencer opened his eyes to the brilliance, and at that moment the comforter slipped from her shoulders, tumbling like a crumbled wall around her. She was glorious against the sky. He gripped her hips, rearing up to meet her thrust, burying himself, losing himself. Head tossing, body quivering, she shuddered and cried out, collapsing against him as he spilled into her, calling her name, holding her like he never wanted to let her go.

SHOES IN HAND, Georgia crept into the house like a thief in the night—only it was eight o'clock in the morning. Jasmine and Emily were standing in the front hall.

"Emily," Georgia sputtered, "what are you doing here?"

"I came to pick up some stuff I forgot." Emily's gaze suddenly seemed to take in her mother's dress. "Kind of fancy for an early-morning trip to the grocery store." She looked at her mother's hands. "Where is it?"

Georgia frowned. "Where's what?"

"The milk Jasmine said you went to the store for."

"Oh." Georgia ran a hand distractedly through her hair, dislodging a few stray gardenia petals. She watched them float to her feet in slow motion. "Guess I forgot the milk," she finally answered.

Emily grinned. "Guess you forgot to get dressed, too."

"Emily—" Georgia began.

Emily crossed her arms. "Did I look as guilty and messed up as you do when I came home at four in the morning? Really, Mom, I thought moving out would give *me* freedom, but it looks like you're the one having all the fun."

"I had car trouble?" Georgia offered meekly.

Emily shook her head. "Try again."

"I took a wrong turn and ended up in Chicago where I got stuck in morning rush-hour traffic?"

Emily grinned wickedly. "Better."

Knowing Emily was enjoying her discomfort, Georgia grinned back, giving it another shot. "How about I was abducted by aliens and I don't remember the last ten hours of my life?" As she said it, she almost wished it were true.

Emily laughed. "Creative, at least. But I never would have had the guts to try that one."

"And I would never be stupid enough to buy it."

"Well, neither would I, Mom. I just figure it's really none of my business where you were all night."

But it is, Georgia had on the tip of her tongue, *because I did it for you. And when you hear where I was and who I was with, you won't want him anymore.* But the tip of her tongue stayed still. Why did Emily have to be so damn mature about finding her mother sneaking home after being out all night? Maybe faced with a little adversity, Georgia would have blurted out in anger where she had been all night. The deed would be done. Mission accomplished.

The only problem was, the words, even spoken in her head, no longer rang true.

Emily picked up a carton and headed for the door. But Georgia couldn't let her go—not like this.

"Emily?" she called.

Emily paused at the door. "Yeah?"

"Is it okay if I come over later—see your studio? And I want to see the piece you've been working on—the one you just sold."

Emily grinned. "Sure, Mom, I'd like that. Maybe we can grab a burger or something—your treat."

Georgia smiled through the lump in her throat. In some ways Emily was still a kid—her kid. "Okay, I'll see you later."

"Better make it much later. By the looks of you, wherever you spent the night, you didn't get much sleep."

Georgia's mouth dropped open, but Emily just laughed and breezed out the door.

"Why didn't you tell her?" Jasmine asked.

Georgia didn't pretend not to know what Jasmine was talking about. "I don't know, Mother. I just couldn't."

Jasmine reached up and patted Georgia's cheek. "Go get some sleep, love—it will all sort itself out in time, you'll see."

But as Georgia wearily climbed the stairs, she doubted that things would ever be sorted out. She had spent the night with Spencer Foxworth and nothing was ever going to be the same again.

Chapter Ten

The ringing telephone pulled Georgia reluctantly from sleep. She opened her eyes, squinting at the light-filled room. Moaning, she screwed her eyes up against the assault and burrowed deeper into the pillow. The phone kept ringing. Fumbling for it, she croaked into the receiver with a sleep-roughened voice. "Hello?"

"Hi, sleepyhead. Still in bed?"

Her mind remained in a fog, but her body was instantly awake. More than awake. Alive. That lazy low voice in her ear shot right through her. Snatches of the night before played before her eyes, and it was suddenly hard to breathe, suddenly too hot.

"Georgia, sweetheart, are you still with me?"

"Uh, yeah—I'm still here."

"When do I get to see you again?" Spencer drawled, and Georgia melted into the bed.

Her body screamed, *Now! Get over here!* But her mind, that sensible instrument, battled to the forefront, emerging victorious as usual. "I can't today—family plans."

"Tonight, then?"

His voice flowed over her like thick honey, satiating every pore. Fighting the sweet lethargy, she managed to say, "Umm, not tonight, either. Sorry."

Spencer groaned. "Come on, Georgia, you're not going to make me wait till Monday, are you?"

Her mind clung to reason on a fine thread. "Monday's a holiday."

"A holiday!" Spencer growled into the phone. "What holiday?" he demanded.

"Memorial Day. It's the end of May, remember?"

She heard the smile in his voice. "I'm having trouble remembering anything, George—anything but last night...."

His voice trailed off on a husky note, and Georgia bit down hard on her lip for control, certain she could hear his deepened breathing in the silence that followed. Then he sighed, a sound cloaked in unhappy resignation. "I suppose I gave you Monday off, then?"

"Standard procedure, boss," Georgia forced herself to say breezily.

Spencer groaned again. "Well, I'm not waiting until Tuesday. You can't ask that of me, George. Tomorrow—you're seeing me tomorrow."

Georgia shut her eyes and started to knead her forehead with shaky fingers. "I don't know, Spencer. I—"

"Tomorrow," he cut in emphatically. "I'll call you." And then he hung up.

Georgia rolled onto her stomach and buried her face in a pillow, wondering what she'd gotten herself into. Some spell had been cast over her last night, making her forget why she was there. No, worse. It had made her begin to doubt.

Had Spencer been after Emily or not? That was the question. If so, it had certainly proved easy to distract him. The notorious womanizer appeared to have fallen like a ton of bricks. And all those comments by certain members of the T-Squares last night: *So glad to see you together at last. Spencer has spoken so often about you....*

And then after the party—

Georgia threw back the covers and headed for the shower.

The cold spray was torture against her skin. Still she felt so hot. When was this heat wave going to break?

But Georgia knew it wasn't just the heat wave making her temperature rise. She soaped her body with her bare hands, and memories seemed to rise from her flesh. Spencer's lean, hard body had been a revelation. And so had his tenderness. He knew just how to touch her, just where to touch her, just when to touch her. Alone in her shower, she blushed at the thought of how wild, how eager she had been on the balcony that morning.

She hadn't known it could be like that, hadn't known *she* could be like that. In her brief, failed marriage, sex had never been important to her, and there hadn't been any men who had gotten that close since. She was the classic case of never having known what she was missing.

But now she did.

Last night, Spencer had opened her up to feelings and possibilities she'd never imagined. How was she ever going to forget? How was she going to turn away from that and go back to what she had been? Because that was the plan. And the plan seemed to have worked.

She'd gotten Spencer's mind off Emily. Now all that remained was to expose him to Emily, because Emily surely would want no part of him once she knew he'd spent the night with her mother.

The image of her daughter standing in the front hall that morning swam into Georgia's mind. She stepped directly under the pulsating shower, lifting her face to the punishing spray. But it was no use, the image wouldn't go away—the nagging question wouldn't go away.

Why, when she'd had the perfect opportunity, delivered gift-wrapped by fate, had she stayed silent? Why hadn't she told Emily?

And this morning on the balcony, why hadn't she told Spencer when he'd asked? Why hadn't she thrown it in his face in triumph, crowing that she'd outfoxed him at his own game?

Maybe I'm falling in love with you.

His words haunted her. She was aware that at that point he'd had no reason to lie, he'd already gotten her into his bed. So much of what had passed between them since she'd started all this didn't fit with the image she'd always held of him, the image she'd insisted on holding for ten years. If he meant those words he'd uttered to the sound of the waves that morning, then what she had done had the power to hurt him. If he meant those words, then she was far worse than she'd ever imagined him to be. Far worse.

But she couldn't think of all that now. Now she had to go see Emily, to see Emily's work. She was getting a second chance with her daughter and she intended to take it.

Out of the shower, Georgia pulled open her closet and started to grab from the colorful section holding her new clothes. She stopped, hand in midair. She moved her hand over to the other side, letting it hover above the older, drab garments that hung there. She could go back to the way things were supposed to be now. She could go back to dressing how she always had.

But she didn't want to. It was still so hot. The new clothes were lighter, more comfortable. She'd wear them just a little longer. Just until this heat wave abated, she told herself. Then things would go back to normal.

GEORGIA PARKED HER CAR across from the gallery, walking to the corner to cross the busy River West area street. Once she hit the far curb, she stopped dead.

No—it couldn't be his. There had to be hundreds of black Jaguars in the Milwaukee area. Slowly she started down the side street, stopping in front of the sleek, low car. She squeezed her eyes shut for a second, then bent down to peer in the passenger window.

There, on the seat where he always left them, were his sunglasses.

Georgia straightened. But there had to be thousands of Ray●Bans like that in the Milwaukee area.

Right?

Of course.

It was only a coincidence that there was a car just like Spencer's parked outside the obscure River West gallery where her daughter was renting a studio. And it was just another coincidence that the driver of said car, whoever he was, had the same taste in eye wear. And a further coincidence that he just happened to have a friend—probably another artist, given the area of town—in the neighborhood.

Given what Spencer had said that morning, what he had done the night before, how he couldn't seem to wait to see her again— given all that, even if he had been after Emily, he certainly wasn't after her any longer.

Nobody—not even Spencer Foxworth—could be that big a rat.

Georgia started to walk away, but something, some undertone of suspicion, made her look back. What her gaze honed in on was what she'd avoided looking at before: the license plate.

FOX.

It was no coincidence. Because no two people in all of Wisconsin would have the same vanity plates. Hell, no two people in all the world would have the vanity to put FOX on their plates, even if it was an abbreviation of their name. No one would have the conceit, the audacity, the sheer ego—no one but Spencer Foxworth!

Georgia marched around the corner and into the building. Ignoring the gallery, she ran all the way up to the second floor, stopping at the only door on the landing. It had to be Emily's.

"Emily, open up," she demanded, pounding on the door with her fist. When there was nothing but silence from within, she kicked at the door with her foot. "I know you're in there—I know *he's* in there. Now open this door!"

The door creaked slowly to reveal Emily's eye through a tiny slit.

"Mom, for heaven's sake. What's the matter?"

"Let me in and I'll tell you what's the matter. I should have told you this morning—but no, that swine almost had me bamboozled into believing him. Emily, he's been using me—he's been using you. Now let me in there so I can strangle him!"

Emily reluctantly widened the opening, enough for Georgia to see that her shirt was buttoned wrong, her hair was a mess, her lipstick was chewed off.

Georgia groaned and buried her face in her hands. "I'm too late, aren't I?"

"Too late for what? Mom, I think you've finally lost it. What are you talking about?"

"He's in there, isn't he? And you two have just—" Georgia choked on the words. There was no way she could say them out loud.

"Well yes, he's here...." Emily stood up straighter, her mouth tightening. "But I refuse to discuss what we've just done, *or* if we've just done it for that matter. I'm twenty years old. Who I do what with is none of your business."

"Even if the who you just did what with is the who I did what with just last night?"

Emily's face screwed up. "Huh?"

"Ask him where he was last night. Go on, ask him."

Emily looked briefly over her shoulder, shrugged, then looked back at Georgia. "Mom, he was with me last night."

"Oh, come on. Even Spencer Foxworth couldn't perform that well!"

"Who?"

But Georgia had lost all patience. She pushed at the door until it was open, then she pushed past Emily and into the studio.

And there he was, the snap of his tight jeans undone, his chest bare, his head hiding under the T-shirt he was struggling to fit over his head.

She stalked over to him. "You coward. You swine. You—you—" She grabbed the T-shirt, yanking it down. "You absolute—" her mouth fell open. "Vinnie!"

"Absolutely," Vinnie said with an uncomfortable grin.

And it was Vinnie, all right. But where was Spencer?

"Where is he?"

Vinnie and Emily looked at each other. "Where's who?"

"Spencer Foxworth, that's who."

Emily crossed her arms. "How should I know?"

"But his car—it's parked out there."

Emily threw her arms up. "Well, he's not here. You're welcome to look under the bed if you don't believe me."

Georgia suddenly realized the absurdity of the situation. Unless Spencer *was* hiding under the bed, Georgia was wrong, Georgia was a fool, and Georgia was getting out of here—now.

"I'm sorry, Emily—really sorry. Just—just forget I was here," she stammered, slamming the door behind her.

Georgia stood on the landing, trying to catch her breath. Emily and Vinnie? Well, why not? She'd always liked Vinnie. He was nice, decent, talented. A little old for Emily, but not as old as—

What was going on? Where was Spencer? Had it been Vinnie all along? But she'd seen Spencer bring Emily home that night with her own eyes. She'd heard them talking on the phone together.

Well, no, that wasn't precisely true. She'd just assumed—

Had she assumed it all? Imagined it all? What about the sculpture? Georgia knew for a fact that Spencer had bought it. Even now, Emily was living off the spoils.

The sculpture seemed to be the key. Georgia ran down the stairs to the gallery.

"MY GOD, IS THAT IT? Is that Emily's?"

Spencer hadn't heard her come in, but when he recognized her voice, he grinned at his own reaction. It was immediate, that rush of desire and happiness that she was here.

He turned and went to her. "It's hers. Come and see it."

Georgia took his hand and let him lead her forward.

"This is *Moondancer,*" Spencer whispered, and the hushed tone of his voice did not strike Georgia as strange at all. The piece had power—it stilled her, captured her senses.

"I had no idea," she whispered back. "No idea at all."

Spencer squeezed her hand. "I told Emily that if you saw it, it would make a difference in how you felt."

At the mention of Emily's name, Georgia pulled her hand out of his. "Why did you buy it?" she demanded.

"Just look at it. It's a wonderful first piece. She's good, Georgia. Surely you can see that now."

Georgia nodded dumbly. "But is that the only reason you bought it?"

Spencer looked at her oddly, taking a moment to answer. "I guess if I were honest, I'd have to say no."

"Aha!" Georgia bellowed in triumph, even though something hollow seemed to fall from her heart to her stomach.

"Aha?" Spencer's eyes narrowed. "What's that supposed to mean?"

"Then you admit that you bought it to get at Emily. You admit that you wanted her to have the money to move out of my house to make it easier for you and her to—to—"

"Are you crazy? What are you talking about?"

"You've been after my daughter. Don't try to deny it, you rat. Fortunately, it seems she had the good sense to stay away from you."

Spencer shook his head. "George, I don't know what you're talking about. The other reason I bought *Moondancer* is because it reminds me of you."

Georgia almost stumbled on that one. "What?"

"She has fire and ice, hardness and flow. She's larger than life, yet somehow vulnerable, waiting. She's you, George, and I wanted her for my own."

He started toward her, and she backed away, suddenly afraid of him.

"I'm glad you showed up here today, sweetheart. There was no way I could wait until tomorrow to see you again."

He kept coming, she kept retreating, until her back hit the wall and there was nowhere else to go. She swallowed. "Umm, Spencer. About last night?"

"Mmm," he moaned, "that's all I can think about. Last night—and this morning."

He had come up close to her now, putting his hands against the wall on either side of her shoulders, trapping her. She started to breathe heavily, telling herself it was fear, telling herself that she didn't really still want him, even though her body throbbed, yearned.

She wet her lips. "About last night?" she croaked. "Could we just forget it ever happened?"

He blinked. "What?"

She tried for a smile but got a grimace instead. "Let's just forget it ever happened, okay? It was just one of those things, you know? Just a—a mistake. Yeah, a mistake."

"You're kidding, right?"

She shook her head wildly.

"Listen, sweetheart, it was no mistake and it was unforgettable. Let me refresh your memory."

His hands came off the wall and gripped her shoulders. He pulled her into him, laying a kiss on her that threatened to make her mind go blank, let alone remember anything. Georgia almost swooned. Her arms came up and around him, her body settled into his, and she kissed him back.

But only for a second. Then she remembered that it was over and she didn't have to go through any more of this—this—this—what? Ecstasy? Joy?

No. Pretense. She didn't have to go on with this pretense.

She pushed him away. "No."

He raked his hand through his hair. "You're right," he said through heaving breaths. "Not here. Let's go out to the house. We can pick up your car later—much later."

He started to reach for her hand, but she jumped out of his reach.

"I meant no, not just here. Not anywhere. I—I don't want to see you again. Except—except at work," she sputtered, wondering how she was ever going to be able to work with him again after this.

"George, sweetheart, what are you saying?"

"I—I'm saying that last night was a mistake. It isn't going to happen again. It didn't happen, so forget it, okay?" She started for the door as fast as her shaking legs could carry her. "And don't call me George," she yelled over her shoulder.

GEORGIA RAN INTO the house, slammed the door behind her and locked it, then leaned back against it, breathing like she'd just run a race with the bogeyman.

"Georgia, love, is something wrong?"

"Everything, Mother. Everything in the whole world is wrong." She turned around and lifted the edge of the lace curtain on the door, peering out, half expecting to see the black Jag race up to the curb. She had this horrible feeling that the man was after her. And who could blame him.

Jasmine glided up behind her. "Is someone out there?"

Georgia jumped and spun around. "No, thank God."

Jasmine looked amused. "Who were you expecting?"

"Spencer Foxworth, that's who," Georgia answered, walking heavily past her and into the living room.

Jasmine followed. "I thought you were going to the gallery."

"I was. I did." Georgia sat in a wing-backed chair, leaned her head back and closed her eyes. "I've been wrong," she said. "Terribly wrong." She opened her eyes and looked at Jasmine. "She's really good, isn't she?"

Jasmine nodded. "More than good. It's a powerful piece, especially from a novice. She'll make a name for herself one day, George, one day soon. Now that she's taken the plunge, there'll be no stopping her."

"You mean, now that she's broken away from me, don't you? Now that I won't be there to try to run her life? God, I've made so many mistakes—"

"So have we all, George, my love. So have we all."

Georgia got up and went to the kitchen. She filled a glass with water, took it to the screen door and stood looking out at the sky. The sun was finally gone, but if anything, the air was warmer, thicker. It would rain soon and maybe that would wash away some of the humidity, some of the heat. Georgia wished a storm would come, one big enough, violent enough, to wash away the last few days.

"You're not happy for her, are you?" Jasmine asked from the doorway.

Georgia sighed. "Of course I am, Mother. I'm not that big a monster. I wouldn't wish her to have no talent just so I could be right."

"I never thought you were a monster, George. I just thought you'd be happier once you knew that Emily made the right choice. You see that now, don't you?"

"I seem to be the only one making the wrong choices." She closed her eyes again, leaning her head against the screen. "What am I going to do, Mother? What am I going to do?"

"About Emily? But I thought—"

"No." Georgia pulled away from the door. "Not Emily. Spencer. What am I going to do about Spencer Foxworth? How am I going to go on working for him, spending time with him every day after—after—"

Jasmine's eyes twinkled. "After what, George?" she asked innocently.

"You know very well after what, Mother. Don't make me say it!" Another thought struck her. "Maybe he'll fire me and I'll never have to see him again."

"Fire you? For what—sleeping with him? I think there are laws against that sort of thing, George."

Georgia rolled her eyes. "Not for sleeping with him—for lying to him, for deceiving him, for believing that he was ever after Emily in the first place."

"Ahh." Jasmine nodded sagely. "I take it that's one of the things you were wrong about."

"Boy, was I."

"And that doesn't make you happy?"

Georgia's forehead puzzled into a frown as she thought it over. Why wasn't she happy about it? Should she be? "Well, yeah, I'm happy about that," she mumbled as she walked back into the living room.

Jasmine followed, shrugging delicately. "Then what's the problem?"

"The problem is the man thinks he may be in love with me. The problem is he wants more of—more of— Well, just more. The problem is now that I've got him, I don't know what to do with him!"

Jasmine chuckled. "Some problem."

"It's not funny! You got me into this, Mother. Now you're going to have to help me get out of it."

"*I* got you into it?"

"Yes, you. You're the one who put the notion of going after him myself in my head. You're the one who said the right woman could keep his mind off Emily. You're the one who—"

"And you're the one who went after him," Jasmine interrupted. "With gusto, I might add. You might examine the fact, love, that embarking on such a plan was hardly second nature to you and yet you managed to do it with very good results. Maybe it's time you asked yourself why a woman whose byword has always been *caution* was willing to go to such lengths."

Georgia frowned. "What's your point, Mother? Just spit it out—I'm too tired for guessing games."

"I'm trying to point out," Jasmine continued calmly as she walked to the living room window and peered out, "what I tried to point out from the very first. Maybe you want the man for yourself—maybe you have all along."

"Hogwash, Mother. I don't want any man for myself—and certainly not a man like Spencer Foxworth."

"Then you really do have a problem, love, because at this very moment Spencer Foxworth is on his way up the front walk." She turned and surveyed Georgia with amusement. "Looks like you've got him whether you want him or not."

Chapter Eleven

Spencer took the front steps to Georgia's house two at a time. She wasn't getting away with this. For the first time in his life he was hooked, caught, truly and fully in love. And he wasn't running away from it. He wasn't going to let her run away from it, either.

Laying a thumb on the doorbell, he bellowed, "Georgia! I know you're in there! Let me in!" Maybe the doorbell wasn't working. He started to pound. "Georgia," he yelled between wallops, "I'm not going away until you open this door!"

The door opened.

"Okay, I opened the door, now go away."

But before Georgia could shut it again, Spencer placed a foot on the threshold.

Georgia fumed. "Who do you think you are, a vacuum-cleaner salesman?"

"I'm the man you spent the night with and I want an explanation."

Georgia gave up and let go of the door. She might as well have it out with him now. "Just because we— Just because we—"

"Made love, Georgia. What we did was make love."

She gave him a look. "Just because we *had sex* doesn't mean we have a relationship."

"We didn't *have sex*—we made love. And, yes, we do have a relationship. We've had a relationship for ten years, George. I've been falling in love with you for ten years!"

"You're not in love with me—you couldn't possibly be."

"Yes, I am."

"How would you know, anyway? You've never been in love."

"That's how I know."

That stopped her for a moment. "Well—well, I'm certainly not in love with you."

"Sure you are."

"Of all the conceit—"

"Georgia, a woman like you wouldn't go to bed with a man like me unless she's in love."

She tossed her head. "That's ridiculous. Women like me have biological urges just like everyone else."

The corner of his mouth lifted in a grin. "And that's what last night was? A biological urge?"

"Yes." She thrust her chin up. "That's all it was."

He started moving toward her, a wicked gleam in his eye. "Well, I'm starting to get the urge again, George."

She sidestepped his hands. "Well, I'm not."

He reached out and touched her cheek, letting a finger trail down her throat. "I bet it wouldn't take much to get it going, though, would it?"

She jumped back, out of his reach, her heart pounding. "That's your ego talking, Spencer."

"Oh, yeah? Then come over here and we'll give it the test."

She looked at his outstretched hands. A few steps forward and she'd be putty in them—jelly, molten flesh, a mass of heaving hormones.

"I have no intention of testing anything," she replied haughtily. "Now, if you'll excuse me, I have things to do." She turned and marched up the stairs, gripping the banister, hoping that although her knees had turned to water, her legs would hold her up.

"Looks like you've got your work cut out for you," Jasmine said from the living room doorway.

Spencer shook his head. "Your daughter is a nut, you know that?"

Jasmine smiled gently. "Part of her charm is that she thinks she's the only sane one in the world."

Spencer looked worried. "She *is* in love with me, isn't she?"

"I don't doubt it for a minute."

"Then what's her problem?"

"Her problem is, she can't admit it, even to herself. My daughter is not a woman who easily takes chances. Being in love with a man like you is hardly playing it safe. If she hadn't convinced herself that you were after Emily, she never would have had the guts to go after you herself."

Spencer frowned. "Run that by me again?"

"She thought you were going after Emily, and that's why...."

Thrusting his hands in his pockets, Spencer started to pace. She thought he was after Emily, and so she— He chuckled softly. "So that's it," he murmured. It was all becoming clear now. Hadn't she just about told him so at the gallery that afternoon? All that stuff about Emily. He'd just been too flustered at seeing her again for it to sink in. And then she'd thrown him that curve about forgetting last night had ever happened.

"I knew she was up to something—I just couldn't figure out what." He sat on the bottom step of the open staircase, burying his head in his hands, and laughed.

"I'm glad to see you have a sense of humor about this, Spencer."

"Jasmine, it's priceless. When I think of the lengths she was willing to go to—the clothes, the flirting, the—" He looked suddenly at Georgia's mother. "Well, never mind. And then this afternoon at the gallery—she hadn't a clue as to what to do with me now that she had me. What a woman. What a crazy, wonderful, lovable woman."

Smiling serenely, Jasmine glided over and sat down on the step next to him. "So, what are you going to do about it?"

Spencer thought it over for a minute. "I'm going to woo her," he said, rapidly warming to the idea. "I'm going to send her flowers, candy, jewelry. I'm going to do all the things I should have been doing for years. And I'm going to do it all in one weekend because I don't intend to live through another day without her."

THE ROSES CAME at three. Red roses. Two dozen. "I love you," the card said.

The daisies came at four. Mounds of them. "You love me," the card read.

At five, a special courier delivered a long, slim, black velvet box. Georgia opened it to find a cameo pendant hanging from a chain of gold. The card said, "With love to my old-fashioned girl."

At six, a department store delivered a dress box. Among the folds of tissue lay an ivory silk gown, nearly transparent, nearly topless. He'd written on the card, "For the new Georgia—my sexy, wonderful George."

"This is crazy. What's he trying to do?"

"I believe the term he used was woo. He's trying to woo you, George."

"Really, Mother, I can't even imagine Spencer Foxworth using the word."

"Well, he used it."

Georgia lifted the gown from its nest of tissue. It was a gossamer, ethereal creation, managing to be both sexy and innocent at the same time.

Was that how he saw her? Well, she was far from innocent. If he knew what she had done, why she had changed toward him, he certainly would no longer view her that way.

So why didn't she tell him? Why didn't she just pick up the phone and tell him what a scheming, conniving, controlling louse she really was?

The doorbell rang again.

Georgia threw up her hands. "What now, do you suppose?"

She threw open the door to reveal a pizza delivery man holding a large box. "Well, at least he finally sent me something I can use," Georgia muttered, thrusting an overly large tip at the man.

"Umm, lady," he said, thrusting the tip back at her, "I've already been taken care of. Oh, and the guy who sent this said to eat it all—you're gonna need the strength for what's ahead."

Georgia stood in the doorway holding the steaming box, watching the man walk back to his truck. "What do you suppose he meant by that?"

Jasmine twinkled. "I can think of several possibilities."

Georgia looked at her. "You're as bad as he is, you know that?"

Jasmine sighed. "George, why don't you put the man out of his misery? Call him. Tell him you love him."

"But I don't," Georgia insisted on her way to the kitchen. "And quit calling me George!"

An hour later, as Georgia was washing down the last piece of pizza with an ice-cold beer, the doorbell pealed again.

"Oh, no," she moaned. "What could possibly be left for him to send me?"

When she threw open the front door, there stood on her stoop four boys—at least, she thought they were boys—in Beatles wigs, holding ridiculous little plastic guitars. Before she could say a word, they started to shake their mop tops and sing a love song in slightly off-key harmony.

Georgia slammed the door in their collective faces and marched directly for the phone.

"Spencer, you've got to stop this."

"Okay," he said reasonably. "Admit you love me, and I'll stop it."

"No."

"No?"

"Definitely not."

"Okay," he said agreeably, "then I hope you left room for dessert."

She was still staring at the receiver when the doorbell chimed.

"No—I refuse to answer that," she screamed, heading up the stairs and throwing herself on the bed.

Jasmine's voice floated up to her moments later. "Georgia, love, I think you better come down here."

With a kind of dread, Georgia dragged herself off the bed and slowly descended the stairs.

"Oh, no—"

There, in Jasmine's arms, was the biggest, most ostentatiously decorated and most tastelessly done cake Georgia had ever seen. Cherubs and doves abounded. Pink and red roses clashed. Hearts and vines intertwined. And written across the top, in bold red script, was the message "I love you."

"Let's just hope it's chocolate," Georgia muttered, grabbing the cake from Jasmine's arms and heading for the kitchen.

She was in the process of cutting herself a huge slice when Emily walked in.

"Holy cow. Who got married?"

"Nobody—yet," Jasmine replied smoothly.

Georgia gave her a warning look. "Nobody— ever. He only wants me to admit I love him. Nobody said anything about marriage."

Emily grabbed a cake plate and pulled out a chair. "Great. I move out and things start to cook around here," she complained, cutting herself a huge slab of the pink monstrosity. "Who wants you to admit you love him and where did this cake come from?"

"Spencer Foxworth and Spencer Foxworth."

Emily stopped chewing, her mouth dropping open, cake crumbs drifting down the front of her T-shirt. "Spencer?" she gasped. "I knew it. I just knew it!"

Georgia eyed her daughter. "You knew what?"

"I knew he had the hots for you—probably has for years."

"Has the whole world lost its mind?"

"Mom, he practically told me so the day we had lunch together. You should hear the way he defended you."

"You talked about me at that lunch?" Georgia asked meekly.

"We sure did. He told me he'd probably make a pass at you but he figured you'd scream sexual harassment and have him arrested."

"He did not!"

Emily shrugged. "Well, something like that."

"But I thought you and he—"

Emily dropped her fork. "Me and Spencer?" She screwed up her face. "Get real. Oh, I admit the thought occurred to me. I mean, he used to have a reputation for liking them young. But he definitely wasn't interested. Now I know why. He was already in love with you."

"He is not in love with me!"

"Sure he is, Mom. Says so right here on the cake." Emily scooped up a fingerful of shocking pink frosting, sticking it in her mouth.

"It said so on the card with the roses, too," Jasmine put in.

Georgia stood up. "Mother!"

"Roses? Really?" Emily asked.

Jasmine leaned forward, putting her elbows on the table. "Roses and daisies and cameos and lingerie and pizza—"

"Pizza?" Emily looked hopefully around the kitchen.

Jasmine nodded. "Something every hour on the hour."

"Wow, talk about a whirlwind courtship. The man believes in making up for lost time. I guess that's why you weren't too shook about Vinnie and me, huh? I mean, you've got your hands full with a man of your own."

Georgia whirled from the sink where she'd been rinsing dishes. "I do not have a man of my own! And I have absolutely no objection to Vinnie. He's a nice guy. Besides, it's your life, and I would never dream of interfering."

Emily started laughing so hard, she had to hold her hand over her mouth to keep from spitting out a mouthful of cake.

Georgia leaned against the sink and crossed her arms. "What's so funny?"

"You not interfering—hah! It's your middle name, Mom. Georgia Interfering Moon."

"Well, it may have been in the past," Georgia conceded, "but things have changed."

"Boy, I'll say. In love with Spencer Foxworth—that's one big megachange."

"I am not in love with Spencer Foxworth! Now, could we change the subject?"

"To?"

"To your work."

Emily groaned. "I thought you weren't going to interfere anymore."

"I'm not going to. I just want to say..." She took a deep breath. "I just want to say that I saw *Moondancer* today and she's wonderful. You've got a lot of talent, Emily, and I think you're making the right choice to—to quit school and pursue it."

Emily stared at her mother for a moment, then she was on her feet, throwing herself into Georgia's arms. "Do you know how long I've waited to hear those words from you? This is so great! And you really don't mind about Vinnie, either?"

"Well, he is a little old for you—"

Jasmine stood up and joined the circle of women. "But your mother likes him very much and he's welcome in her home. Right, Georgia?"

"Yes. Of course. Right." And Georgia was surprised as she said the words to find that she really meant them. Vinnie was okay. And if her daughter wanted to devote her life to sculpting, that was okay, too. She gave both her daughter and mother one last hug, then pulled away.

The awful cake, taking up half the kitchen table, stared at her. She had problems of her own to worry about. Emily was just going to have to live her own life.

"I'm exhausted. I'm going up to bed."

She kissed Emily good-night and made her way upstairs.

The dress box lay on her bed. After a moment's hesitation, she eased off the lid. The ivory silk nestled in its bed of tissue, looking soft and pretty—and expensive. She lifted it by its thin, silky straps and held it in front of her.

The man knew how to pick out lingerie. It was just the right size, too.

She took it to the mirror, holding it to her body. Gorgeous. What would it hurt to try it on? Who would know?

She shrugged out of her clothes and let the garment float over her body. It rested against her pale skin, whisper soft, dipping low over her breasts, then flowing straight to her toes. It shimmered when she moved, clinging to every curve.

The box from the jewelers sat on her dresser. Her fingers itched to open it. What the heck—who would know if she tried the cameo on, too?

She snapped open the lid. The ivory carving was delicate, feminine, the background a pale honey tone, the gold chain a fine, shiny thread. She slipped it around her neck, and it nestled just above her breasts, gleaming against her pale flesh.

She touched her throat, pushed the hair back from her face and stared at her reflection. She looked— She looked beautiful.

The phone rang, pulling her out of her daze. Automatically, she reached for it.

"Do you have it on?" he murmured in a voice so low, so seductive, her body came alive. Her eyes flew back to the image in the mirror. How did he know?

"Don't tell me you're a mind reader, too."

"Mmm, you do have it on."

Georgia winced at her mistake. "That's none of your business."

"Tell me how it looks, George. Tell me how it feels against your skin."

She trembled lightly, gripping the receiver for balance. "What is this—some kind of obscene phone call?"

"Is that what you'd like?" he asked softly.

"Of course not."

"You know what I'd like, George? I'd like to come over there and see you in it."

"No—"

"Then you come over here."

"No!"

He chuckled. "How was the cake?"

"It was the worst thing I've ever seen. And don't bother to pay that faux pop group you sent over here. I slammed the door in their faces before they finished the first chorus."

Spencer laughed softly. "Just tell me you love me, and I'll stop."

Georgia closed her eyes and groaned. "Don't tell me you've got more surprises planned?"

"Well, there's always tomorrow."

"Spencer, please—"

"Anything you want, sweetheart. I love it when you beg."

Unable to help it, she laughed.

"I love it when you laugh."

"Will you stop!"

"I love you, George."

Georgia swallowed. "No you don't, Spencer. Right now, for some odd reason, you just think you do. You don't really know me. You don't know some of the things I've done."

"And you know *everything* I've done—at least, for the past ten years. I'm no saint, Georgia. I would never judge you."

Wouldn't he, even if he knew?

"Come out with me tomorrow. I'll take you out to the Hawkins site. Thanks to you and the nervous state you've had me in all day, the plans are nearly complete. I want you to see it, sweetheart. I want to share it with you. I want to share my whole life with you."

"Unless you want me to hang up, stop spouting nonsense and tell me about the plans."

So he did. She settled herself on the bed, the silk draping her body, the cameo tickling her breasts, and listened to him talk. She asked questions, gave opinions, argued points. Curled up on the bed, the phone propped at her ear, she found herself wishing it were all real.

"Are you still there, George?"

"Yes," she answered softly.

"See how good we are together? We can talk, we can laugh, we can be honest with each other. And in bed— Ahh, George, if you only knew how much I want you right now."

If only he hadn't said the part about being honest. She sat up straight. "I'm hanging up now, Spencer. Don't call me again tonight. And don't call me George!"

SPENCER REPLACED the receiver on the bedside phone and padded naked out to the balcony. The lake breeze washed over him, dispelling some of the humidity. Heat lightning flashed in the distance. Storm clouds bubbled and churned overhead.

He wanted her here with him now.

When had his feelings for her turned to love? Had he really been falling in love with her for ten years? As he scanned through the pages of his memory, it seemed so.

Of all the women he'd known, Georgia was the one constant in his life. He'd never tired of her—her wit, her intelligence, her acid tongue. And now that he'd tasted her body, he knew he'd never tire of that, either.

But there was something more. Tonight he'd talked about his work like he'd never done with anyone before. And she'd done more than listen. She'd drawn him out, urged him on. She'd argued and laughed. She was a stimulating woman. He wanted her mind here with him as much as he wanted her body.

He turned away from the balcony and looked at his empty bed. Somehow he was going to have to convince her that they belonged together, because he had no intention of spending another night without her.

GEORGIA SPENT a restless night. Every time she thought she was about to drift off, she kept hearing that seductive voice. *Tell me how it looks.... Tell me how it feels against your skin....*

By the time a dismal, cloudy dawn broke, she was worn-out remembering what it felt like against her skin; remembering lying on the bed, listening to him talk, laughing with him, sharing with him; remembering the trip to Grand Avenue Mall, the fun they'd had just looking at books, just reading the crazy greeting cards on a rack.

She swung her feet to the floor and headed for a brisk shower. Just because she had a good time with him didn't mean she loved him. Just because he flew her to the moon every time he touched her didn't mean she loved him. And just because she couldn't sleep for thinking about him didn't mean she loved him.

Georgia Moon was much too sensible to fall in love with a man like Spencer Foxworth.

A short while later, out of the shower and dressed for the day, Georgia paused at Jasmine's open bedroom door on her way to the stairs.

"Mother, what are you doing?"

Jasmine finished tucking something into the open suitcase on her bed before turning to her daughter.

"I guess, in all the excitement yesterday, I forgot to tell you."

Georgia frowned and came into the guest room. "Forgot to tell me what?"

"I'm going to New York. My flight leaves in a few hours."

"New York?" Georgia sank down on the bed. "But why? I mean, why now?"

Jasmine's mouth inched its way into a tiny, secret grin. "Your father called."

Georgia groaned. "He calls and you come running."

"Now, that's not true, George. I refused to visit him in Paris, but he's in New York now and I could do with a round of the galleries, anyway, so—"

"What you could really do with is a round of him."

Jasmine stopped packing and smiled. "That's true," she sighed. "I still love the man, impossible though he may be."

"But how do you know?"

Jasmine looked at her. "How do I know I love him? That's easy. No other man has ever made me feel the way he does. No other man has had the power to make me laugh as he does—or make me as mad as he does. I respect his talent, love his wit— and I can't imagine going through my life without him."

"And that's love?"

Jasmine shrugged. "For me, it is. But I guess there's also something indefinable about it. Your heart just knows—"

Georgia watched Jasmine snap the suitcase shut, feeling something close to panic. "Mother, you can't go. You can't do this to me!"

"Do what to you?"

"You can't leave me at the mercy of that man! With Emily gone and now you—I'll have no protection from him whatsoever!"

Jasmine patted her cheek. "You mean you'll have no protection from *yourself*. Isn't it your generation that coined the phrase, 'If it feels good, do it'?"

Georgia followed her mother down the stairs. "But I've never lived that way!"

"Then maybe it's time you did. Quit being so sensible and take a chance."

"But what if I take a chance and it turns out to be all wrong? What if I take a chance and it doesn't work out?"

Jasmine put her suitcase down in the front hall and turned to her daughter. "Oh, but, Georgia, what if it does?"

Chapter Twelve

"I had no idea there was such a terrific view from your backyard, George."

Georgia craned her head over her shoulder to find Spencer Foxworth grinning at her fanny, pointed heavenward as she knelt digging in the garden. Quickly, she sat back on her heels, wishing she'd decided against the white short shorts and black halter top for the morning's chore of planting the geraniums.

"What are you doing here?" she demanded.

"I'm here to deliver your last present."

"Oh, no. . . ." Georgia stood up, dusting the soil off her bare knees. She had hoped that by avoiding the house, with its ringing phone and chiming doorbell, she'd be able to avoid whatever Spencer had planned for the day. But he'd shown up in person.

"I shudder to think of what atrocity you've got up your sleeve." And it must literally be up his sleeve, she thought. His arms weren't laden with anything and his hands seemed empty. Her gaze scanned the yard, finding nothing.

"Well, where is it?" she asked with unhappy resignation.

He held his arms out to his sides. "Right here, sweetheart. It's me—I'm all yours."

Georgia groaned, but as she looked him over, she had to admit that he did look like a package almost any woman wouldn't mind opening. Dressed all in white, his loose cotton shirt was unbuttoned to its usual degree and tucked into white drawstring pants, also loose, but giving a nice hint of certain hidden attributes just the same. His skin glowed with a healthy tan. His chestnut hair, windblown, hung dashingly over those deep blue eyes.

Gorgeous. Ruggedly adorable. Sexy and sweet. He was just about irresistible. But he was one present that Georgia Moon had absolutely no intention of unwrapping.

"Swell. The discount stores are open today—if I hurry I can trade you in on a nice, efficient weed whacker."

Spencer laughed. "Still resisting your fate, I see." He sighed dramatically and sunk to his knees.

"Guess I'll just have to prove that I'm as efficient as any weed whacker," he said, digging his hands into the soil and grinning up at her rakishly. "And," he added, his dark eyes suggestively scanning her body, "I have other, more creative uses besides. You can do things with me, sweetheart, that would be just too dangerous to do with a weed whacker."

"Something tells me, Spencer, that little could be more dangerous than what you're thinking right at this moment."

"So, live a little dangerously."

Take a chance. Live dangerously. The world was just full of advice today.

And Georgia had no intention of taking any of it. She handed him a trowel. "Get your mind out of the gutter and into the dirt. Work on that section until it's loose enough for planting. I'll get the rest of the geraniums."

Spencer watched her walk to the garage, her legs long and lush, her white shorts hugging her rounded bottom. He'd barely slept the night before, thinking about her, wanting her with him. Today was the day she was going to admit that she loved him. He wasn't sure how he was going to accomplish that task, given her stubborn streak, but he was here, on his knees—maybe not doing what he'd like to do, but it was a start.

He rolled up his sleeves and started to work the soil. By the time Georgia came back with the flat of geraniums, he was ready to plant.

"See, I told you I was efficient."

"Terrific. In fact, you're doing such a great job, I think I'll take a break while you finish up," Georgia said sweetly.

"But...." Spencer watched her walk to the house. Her back and shoulders, left bare by the halter, glistened with a sheen of sweat. He had all he could do to keep from throwing down the trowel and chasing after her, pulling her to a stop and running his tongue down her back, tasting the salt on her flesh, tasting—

He shook his head and picked up a pot of geraniums. Down, boy, he told himself. You've got to give this a little time or you'll find yourself out on your ear before you even get started.

In the kitchen, Georgia poured herself a big glass of ice-cold lemonade and stood at the sink, sipping. Spencer Foxworth was actually on his knees in her backyard, planting flowers. If she played her cards right, maybe she could get him to clean out the rain gutters. She smiled at the thought. Maybe if she gave him enough chores to do he'd run for his life and never come back again. She'd be rid of him for good. By the time she got to work Tuesday morning, he'd be too busy nursing his blistered fingers and aching back to think about lusting after her.

She poured a second glass of lemonade and headed back out.

"Good job, Spencer. I see you're already finished."

"Yup." He stood and brushed off his pants. "Piece of cake."

She handed him the lemonade. "You'll need this."

He grinned at her. "Thanks, sweetheart." He gulped the cold liquid, wiping his forehead on the back of his hand, surveying the clouds brewing overhead. "Let's hope that storm comes soon and sends this heat wave packing."

"Well, I hope for your sake, Spencer, it doesn't come too soon," she said sweetly.

"Why is that?"

"I'd hate to see you get struck by lightning while you're cleaning out the gutters."

"Cleaning out the—" But she was already headed for the house.

"Come on," she called over her shoulder. "I'll show you where the ladder is."

Half an hour later, he was still at it, scooping twigs, leaves and some squirrel's forgotten hoard of acorns out of Georgia's gutters. The thunder rumbled closer, lightning flashed in the distance. Occasionally, solitary drops of rain spattered his arms.

"How are we doing?"

Spencer looked down to find Georgia smiling sweetly up at him. "*We're* doing fine. But *we're* going to need a hell of a lot more than a glass of lemonade when *we're* done."

"Anything you say, Spencer," she replied provocatively. "I'll go fix you a sandwich."

"That wasn't exactly what I had in mind," he called after her retreating back. But he couldn't help but laugh. The woman was a challenge. She certainly was.

Georgia placed a plate of roast-beef sandwiches next to a bowl of pasta salad, then glanced out into the yard. She figured Spencer would seize any chance to come down off that ladder. After all, he was the man who designed houses, not built them. Probably never got his hands dirty. And those clothes... Georgia chuckled to herself. He certainly hadn't come over here dressed for yard work.

Big splashes of rain hit the window above the sink. It was only a matter of time before the deluge would start. A crack of lightning spiked through the sky, closer than anything yet, the rumble of accompanying thunder loud and ominous.

Spencer shouldn't be up on that ladder. The joke had gone far enough. She wanted to punish him, true, for invading her existence, for edging his way into her heart, but she certainly didn't want the man fried to a crisp by a bolt of lightning.

She hurried out the back door.

He wasn't on the ladder.

"Spencer," she called.

"Up here," he answered.

She backed away from the house and looked up.

"What on earth are you doing on the roof?"

"You've got a couple of shingles loose up here. I found some extras and a hammer in the garage."

"Spencer, get down from there. A storm's coming, for heaven's sakes. You're a human lightning rod up there."

He peered over the edge of the roof, grinning wolfishly. "Worried about me, sweetheart?"

Georgia put her hands on her hips. "Worried about my insurance premiums."

Spencer laughed and started down the ladder. "Roof's all done, gutters are clean. Anything else I can do for you, sweetheart?"

Georgia frowned. "Why so affable? You never struck me as the kind of man who liked household chores. In fact," she added, looking at the hammer in his hands, "I'm surprised you even know how to use one of those things."

"I learned about designing houses from the bottom up. Worked on a construction crew summers while I was in college." He hefted the hammer. "Feels kind of good to get back into it. Besides, I figure you'll be putting the house up for sale soon. Better have it in good shape."

Georgia's mouth dropped open. "Up for sale? Why would I want to sell my house?"

Spencer threw the hammer on the ground and started toward her. "Well, sweetheart, after you marry me, I just naturally assumed we'd be living at my place."

"Marry you? Live at your place? You and me?"

"Sure." He grinned. "No gutters to clean."

Before Georgia could come up with an answer to that, Spencer pulled her into his arms and lowered his mouth to hers.

It wasn't a friendly kiss. There was pent-up passion there and it swept her into its wake. Her mouth opened to his and he groaned into the kiss, his hands moving up and down her back, fitting their bodies together. Trembling, she clutched at his shirt. He tore his mouth from hers, his breath coming in gasps, the words coming between the furious kisses he rained down her neck.

"God, you taste good—you feel good. I've missed you, George. Don't ever make me wait this long again."

His mouth came down on hers again, knocking what little breath she had out of her lungs, giving her no chance to protest when his fingers found her breast. My God, she wanted him. She wanted him right now—

He dragged her down to the ground, the earth warm and damp beneath them, the sweet smell of crushed grass rising in the heavy air. His tongue swept across her lips as his hand inched beneath the halter. She caught her breath and opened her eyes.

The sky above them was filled with the storm. Soft rain wet her face; she felt the rumble of thunder through the earth. His body was heavy against her, his hand on her breast, touching, teasing. She needed to stop him. She needed to remember that they were in her backyard. She needed to remember that it was still daylight.

But all she really wanted to do was close her eyes and surrender—to the storm, to the love.

But she couldn't. She opened her mouth to protest, but his lips crushed hers again, his dancing tongue almost making her forget what she'd wanted to say.

She pushed at his shoulders, twisting her mouth away from his. "Spencer—stop. For heaven's sakes, we're in my backyard. I have neighbors," she blurted out, and Spencer finally pulled away, sprawling onto his back, his chest heaving with laughter, the rain streaming down his face.

"It's not funny," Georgia huffed, sitting up and adjusting her damp clothing, looking around furtively. It'd be just her luck if her neighbors had suddenly acquired a penchant for barbecuing in the rain. But all was quiet except for Spencer's irritating chuckle.

"What is so funny?"

"You are." He looked at her, wiping his eyes. "You didn't seem to mind making love in *my* backyard," he drawled, running a finger along the curve of her breast. "In fact, if memory serves me correct, you were damn eager for it, Ms. Moon, and not exactly quiet about it, either."

She pushed his hand away and stood up, dashing at the grass stains on the seat of her shorts. "You don't have a backyard, Mr. Foxworth, and you don't have neighbors."

"True." He rolled onto his side, propping his head in one hand. With the other hand he grabbed her leg, running it up and down the smooth, pale skin. "So why don't we go back to my place. We can stand on the balcony, naked in the rain, and make love all night long.''

The image was electrifying. So was his touch, his slightly callused hand moving farther up her thigh. If she gave herself just a little push, she'd be beside him again, quenching the raging storm rolling in the lower regions of her belly. If she gave herself a little push— But she wasn't going to.

"I have no interest in ever making love with you again," she replied haughtily.

Spencer raised a brow mockingly and jumped to his feet. "Really?"

"Yes, really. From now on, please refrain from pawing at me."

Spencer looked down at himself. "Looks like I wasn't the only one doing the pawing."

That was when Georgia noticed the smudges of dirt on the front of his shirt, left there by her own eager hands, and the vertical tear with its enticing view of male breast peaking through. Georgia groaned and covered her eyes with her hand.

Spencer pulled the hand from her eyes. "Hey, sweetheart, don't worry about it." He raised the hand to his mouth, but instead of kissing it he sucked lightly at the tips of her fingers.

Georgia had all she could do to keep standing.

"I like you wild and eager," he said, his eyes boring into her. Nipping lightly at her fingers, he released them, treating her to a devastating grin, the one she seemed to have run out of antibodies for. "Come on, Ms. Moon, let's get out of the rain so you can finish ripping my clothes off."

Dumbly, she let him lead her into the house. Once inside she came to her senses before he could kiss her again, and pulled her hand away from his.

"There's—there's still work to do, Spencer. And if you're not going to help me, then you had better leave."

Spencer sighed. "Okay, slave driver. What's next?"

She thought fast. "The basement. I have a bunch of junk down in the storage room I need to sort out and get rid of."

"Okay," he said, grabbing half a sandwich off the plate, "lead the way."

Spencer followed her down the basement steps, munching his sandwich, watching her hips swaying in the brief white shorts. His eyes moved up to her back, bare almost to the waist. All he'd have to do was reach out and pull the little bow that held the halter up and—

He had to duck his head to enter the storage room. Shelves lined the walls, piled with dozens of cartons. "You're not planning on going through all of these today, are you?"

She gave him an innocent look. "Why not?"

"Because I can think of much better things to do." He reached for her, but she sidestepped him neatly.

"I told you, I have work to do. Either help or leave." Georgia practically held her breath, hoping he'd be disgusted enough to go.

"Okay. What do you want me to do?"

She looked at the shelves. Actually, the last thing she wanted to do was clean the basement, but she'd started this.... "Well—"

Thunder crashed just overhead and the light hanging from the low ceiling flickered. The rain picked up quickly, driving a beat against the house.

"Looks like it's broken at last," Spencer murmured. The windowless storage room was cool, dim. He could think of worse places to be with Georgia Moon. If only she had something besides cleaning in mind. If only he could convince her that she loved him, that they belonged together. He'd have made love to her right here on the cement floor if he'd thought it would do any good.

Then he spied the skeleton key in the scarred wooden door. Hands on hips, he stared at it. "Georgia?"

"Hmm?"

"I love you. Will you marry me?"

Georgia looked at him. That had to be the weirdest, most dispassionate proposal she'd ever heard. And why was he staring at the door?

"Of course I won't marry you."

"Why not?"

"I don't love you."

"You sure?"

He still hadn't looked at her. "Y-yes, I'm sure."

"Okay—you asked for it." He slammed the door shut, turning the key in the lock.

"Spencer, what on earth—?"

He held the key aloft triumphantly. "I intend to keep you my prisoner until you see reason. Until you realize that you love me and we belong together."

"Don't be silly, Spencer." She held out her hand. "Give me the key."

He shook his head and grinned. "Nothing doing. Unless, of course, you're willing to marry me to get it."

"I'd rather starve," she replied dramatically.

"Don't play fast and loose with that word, Georgia. Before this day is out, that pink cake might start looking pretty good to you."

"I'd rather choke than eat one more cherub."

"An empty threat, considering that you're trapped down here with me and the cake is up there in your kitchen."

Georgia's stomach growled. Traitor, she thought. She hadn't even felt hungry until she knew food was out of reach.

"Spencer, this has gone on long enough. Hand over that key."

She started for him, trying to grab the key from his hand, but he was quicker. Before she knew what was happening, he was on the other side of the small room, stooping over the drain in the floor.

"Spencer—no!" she yelled, but too late. There was a ping of metal hitting metal and the key was gone.

"Are you nuts?"

"Nuts about you," he said, stalking toward her.

"Spencer, this isn't funny. We could be stuck down here for days. We could suffocate before anyone comes looking for us!"

"Jasmine will be around. She'll let us out—but hopefully, not before I've made you see reason."

"Jasmine will not be around. Jasmine is gone. She left for New York this morning."

"Oh."

"Yeah, oh. Now, what? Do we perish together like Romeo and Juliet or are you prepared to break down that door?"

Spencer rapped on the door. "Pretty solid. Nice and sturdy. No, I don't think I'll be breaking it down."

"Well, you better figure out a way to get us out of here 'cause I don't intend—"

Thunder rumbled and built, ending in one violent clap directly overhead. The bare bulb flickered again, caught, then died completely.

"Oh, fine. The electricity just went out. Not only am I stuck in this dusty, damp, cramped storage room with a maniac, but now I'm stuck in the dark besides."

"Sounds good to me," Spencer murmured near her ear.

Georgia jumped. "You just keep your distance, Spencer. I don't want any funny business."

"Now, what are we going to do for hours, maybe days, all alone in the dark, if we don't do a little funny business?" he asked, just before she felt his lips at her temple.

She closed her eyes, moaning inwardly, as his mouth moved down her cheek, lightly, softly, inexorably.

"Spencer," she groaned.

"Hmm?"

"Stop."

"Do you really want me to, sweetheart?"

She nodded furiously, but did nothing to put him off. "We have to—stop, I mean."

"Why, Georgia? Why? You know you want me."

Like a phantom of the dark, sent for the sole purpose of tormenting her, he flicked a finger lightly over her breast. Her nipple came alive, hardening, throbbing for more.

She moaned again and turned toward him, offering her mouth in the darkness.

He found it.

She pulled back from the kiss almost immediately. "No, I can't do this."

But he wouldn't let her move away from him. "Why, Georgia?" he asked again in a desperate whisper, pulling her into his arms, holding her gently.

"Because women like me don't have affairs with their bosses."

"Georgia, I meant it when I asked you to marry me. I don't want a quick affair—I want a lifetime."

"That's crazy, Spencer. It couldn't possibly work. We're too different. We're too stubborn."

"It could, baby, it could. We'll both learn to compromise. I'll build a few walls, you'll tear a few down." His arms tightened. "Think of it, Georgia."

His voice was too hypnotic to fight. Georgia closed her eyes, laying her head against his damp shirt, feeling the heat of his body, the beat of his heart.

"Think of it...." He went on in that same low, hypnotic voice. "You and me, long nights together, touching, loving. And not only nights, Georgia, but days. Long summer Sunday afternoons...."

And his phantom hands ran over her, the sound of her catching breath mingling with the beat of the rain.

His voice dipped even lower. "Have you ever made love on the beach, Georgia?"

Georgia swallowed hard and shook her head.

"In the sand, the water's edge, where it's hard and cool, and the waves can wash over your toes. I'll take your clothes off slowly, piece by piece. Can you feel it? Feel the lake breeze on your skin?"

She nodded furiously.

"We can stand naked in the water, Georgia, cool waves lapping our bodies, warmth everywhere we touch."

"I saw you," she whispered.

"What, sweetheart?"

"I saw you in the water one morning—naked."

He smiled, his hand moving down to stroke her backside, his fingers wandering up the leg of her shorts. "If I'd only known you were there, I wouldn't have been swimming alone."

"Alone?" Her mind, overwhelmed by the sensations shooting through her, grappled with that vaguely. Surely he hadn't been alone?

"Mmm, I always swim alone in the mornings. I never wanted anyone there with me—not until you, Georgia."

His fingers slipped between her legs, edging under the silk that covered her. Georgia moaned softly and bit down on her lip. The darkness was filled with the sound of their breathing, filled with the pounding rain and her pounding heart.

Tell him, her mind screamed. Tell him what a rotten schemer you are. Then he'll leave you alone. Then he'll see that he's not in love with you.

Then he touched her deeper and she was too busy searching for his mouth to tell him anything.

She arched against him, wanting it to never stop, wanting it to be all true. Wanting to tell him that she loved him.

He wrenched his mouth away. "I want to make love to you right here, right now. But say it, baby, just say it."

She wanted it. She wanted him. "I love you, Spencer," she moaned, knowing the words to be true the minute they left her lips.

His arms tightened around her. "Oh, Georgia, Georgia. We're going to have one hell of a marriage, you know that? We're going to work together, build beautiful houses, maybe even houses with walls. We're going to have fun together, more fun than you ever had in your entire life. And we're going to make love—we've got ten long years to make up for."

"Spencer?" she said in a small little voice.

"Mmm?"

"There's something I have to tell you. Something you should know before—well, before anything else happens between us."

"Sweetheart, nothing you could tell me would make me change my mind about you. I promise."

"This might."

"Never. But go ahead, anyway. Get it off your chest—and then I'm going to get this little thing you're wearing off your chest, and—"

"Spencer, just listen, okay?"

"Shoot."

"It's about Emily and why—well, why—"

"Oh, you mean the part about how you went after me with a vengeance to save your daughter's virtue?"

Georgia pulled out of his arms. "You know?" she cried.

"Of course I know."

She slapped at the dark in frustration. "You knew all along, you rat, and yet you let me make a complete fool of myself over you! How could you, you—you—"

Her hands flailed in the darkness, whacking him on the chest, the arms, the shoulders. He finally caught them and pulled them to his chest. "Take it easy, sweetheart. I didn't know all along. I mean, I knew you were up to something, but by then I was hooked and I didn't care what it was. Finally, between what you said at the gallery and what Jasmine told me, I put two and two together."

"And you weren't mad that I set out to trick you?"

"Come on, Georgia, you weren't tricking me, you were tricking yourself. We belong together, and thanks to your misguided maternal instinct we finally know it."

She threw her arms around his neck. "Know something, Mr. Foxworth?"

"What, Ms. Moon?"

"Weird as it may seem, I think I really do love you. And, even weirder, I think I do want to marry you and live in your house without walls."

"You don't sound very happy about it."

"What I'm unhappy about is being stuck in this storage room! The air's already getting stale. Any minute now I'm going to start sneezing from the dust, and I'm much too old to make love on a concrete floor."

Spencer smiled. "Does that mean that when we get out of here you're going to take me up to your bedroom and make love to me?"

Georgia sighed. "At this moment, nothing sounds better. Not even a slice of that perfectly ugly cake you sent over last night."

"And you'll wear the silk gown with the cameo?"

Georgia nodded against his neck. "I'll wear anything you want, if only we could just get out of here."

"Wait right here," he said, pulling out of her arms.

She could hear him fumbling near the door. A second later, it swung open.

He stood in the pale light from the doorway, holding the key against his grinning lips.

"You rat! You cheating, you scheming, you—"

"Two of a kind, Georgia. We're two of a kind."

She started to laugh. What else could she do? He was right—they were two of a kind. They belonged together.

"Outfoxed by Foxworth again. What did you throw down the drain?"

"Let's just say that you're going to have to give me a ride home."

She shook her head. "Nothing doing, Foxworth. We have a little business to settle upstairs."

She took his hand, pulling him along, up the basement stairs to the kitchen and through the rest of the house.

Spencer pulled her to a stop just outside the living room. "Just one more thing I'd like to get straight."

"What's that?" Georgia asked.

"When we get married, no more needlepoint pillows. Okay, Georgia?"

"No problem." She grinned. "I have a feeling that I've just found something better to do with my nights. And Spencer?"

"Yes?"

She put her arms around his neck, murmuring against his ear. "You can call me George."

Spencer swung her into his arms and headed up the staircase. "Ahh, George, compromise can be a beautiful thing."

HARLEQUIN

AMERICAN ◆ ROMANCE®

COMING NEXT MONTH

#553 THE MARRYING TYPE by Judith Arnold
Like his friends, Steve Chambliss vowed to be a bachelor forever. Then he appeared on "The Gwen Talbot Show"—and fell hard for the hostess herself. She didn't mix business with pleasure, and confirmed bachelors didn't mix lust with love...or did they? *Don't miss the first book in the Studs series!*

#554 THE INVISIBLE GROOM by Barbara Bretton
More Than Men
Saying "I do" might be the hardest thing Chase Quinn ever had to do—but it was the only way he'd be free of the curse that rendered him invisible. Only thing was, the see-through playboy had to *mean* it!

#555 FINDING DADDY by Judy Christenberry
Kelly Abbott needed a baby—she didn't need or want the man who came along with it. Trouble was, the only guy who met all her requirements—James Townsend—had designs on being a full-time hubby and daddy!

#556 LOVE POTION #5 by Cathy Gillen Thacker
As far as Remy Beauregard was concerned, Jill Sutherland was nothing more than a Yankee career woman with too much attitude—until he accidentally drank a love potion. With every gulp, Jill looked better...until Remy found himself agreeing to a steamy bayou trek. Unfortunately, the antidote Jill sought was now the last thing on Remy's mind.

AVAILABLE THIS MONTH:

#549 THE WEDDING GAMBLE
Muriel Jensen

#550 SEDUCING SPENCER
Nikki Rivers

#551 CRUISIN' MR. DIAMOND
Lynn Leslie

#552 THE PAUPER AND THE PRINCESS
Karen Toller Whittenburg

1994 MISTLETOE MARRIAGES
HISTORICAL CHRISTMAS STORIES

With a twinkle of lights and a flurry of snowflakes, Harlequin Historicals presents *Mistletoe Marriages*, a collection of four of the most magical stories by your favorite historical authors. The perfect way to celebrate the season!

Brimming with romance and good cheer, these heartwarming stories will be available in November wherever Harlequin books are sold.

RENDEZVOUS by Elaine Barbieri
THE WOLF AND THE LAMB by Kathleen Eagle
CHRISTMAS IN THE VALLEY by Margaret Moore
KEEPING CHRISTMAS by Patricia Gardner Evans

Add a touch of romance to your holiday with *Mistletoe Marriages* Christmas Stories!

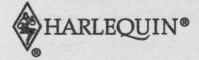

MMXS94

This summer, come cruising with Harlequin Books!

In July, August and September, excitement, danger and, of course, romance can be found in Lynn Leslie's exciting new miniseries PORTS OF CALL. Not only can you cruise the South Pacific, the Caribbean and the Nile, your journey will also take you to Harlequin Superromance®, Harlequin Intrigue® and Harlequin American Romance®.

- ◆ In July, cruise the South Pacific with SINGAPORE FLING, a Harlequin Superromance
- ◆ NIGHT OF THE NILE from Harlequin Intrigue will heat up your August
- ◆ September is the perfect month for CRUISIN' MR. DIAMOND from Harlequin American Romance

So, cruise through the summer with LYNN LESLIE and HARLEQUIN BOOKS!

THE VENGEFUL GROOM
Sara Wood

Legend has it that those married in Eternity's chapel are destined for a lifetime of happiness. But happiness isn't what Giovanni wants from marriage—it's revenge!

Ten years ago, Tina's testimony sent Gio to prison—for a crime he didn't commit. *Now* he's back in Eternity and looking for a bride. *Now* Tina is about to learn just how ruthless and disturbingly sensual Gio's brand of vengeance can be.

THE VENGEFUL GROOM, available in October from Harlequin Presents, is the fifth book in Harlequin's new cross-line series, **WEDDINGS, INC.** Be sure to look for the sixth book, **EDGE OF ETERNITY,** by Jasmine Cresswell (Harlequin Intrigue #298), coming in November.

AMERICAN ROMANCE®

Four sexy hunks who vowed they'd never take "the vow" of marriage...

What happens to this Bachelor Club when, one by one, they find the right bachelorette?

Meet four of the most perfect men:

Steve: **THE MARRYING TYPE**
Judith Arnold
(October)

Tripp: **ONCE UPON A HONEYMOON**
Julie Kistler
(November)

Ukiah: **HE'S A REBEL**
Linda Randall Wisdom
(December)

Deke: **THE WORLD'S LAST BACHELOR**
Pamela Browning
(January)

STUDSG-R

This September, discover the fun of falling in love with...

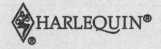

love and laughter

Harlequin is pleased to bring you this exciting new collection of three original short stories by bestselling authors!

ELISE TITLE
BARBARA BRETTON
LASS SMALL

LOVE AND LAUGHTER—sexy, romantic, fun stories guaranteed to tickle your funny bone and fuel your fantasies!

Available in September wherever Harlequin books are sold.

HARLEQUIN®

HARLEQUIN®

Don't miss these Harlequin favorites by some of our most distinguished authors!
And now you can receive a discount by ordering two or more titles!

HT #25525	THE PERFECT HUSBAND by Kristine Rolofson	$2.99	☐
HT #25554	LOVERS' SECRETS by Glenda Sanders	$2.99	☐
HP #11577	THE STONE PRINCESS by Robyn Donald	$2.99	☐
HP #11554	SECRET ADMIRER by Susan Napier	$2.99	☐
HR #03277	THE LADY AND THE TOMCAT by Bethany Campbell	$2.99	☐
HR #03283	FOREIGN AFFAIR by Eva Rutland	$2.99	☐
HS #70529	KEEPING CHRISTMAS by Marisa Carroll	$3.39	☐
HS #70578	THE LAST BUCCANEER by Lynn Erickson	$3.50	☐
HI #22256	THRICE FAMILIAR by Caroline Burnes	$2.99	☐
HI #22238	PRESUMED GUILTY by Tess Gerritsen	$2.99	☐
HAR #16496	OH, YOU BEAUTIFUL DOLL by Judith Arnold	$3.50	☐
HAR #16510	WED AGAIN by Elda Minger	$3.50	☐
HH #28719	RACHEL by Lynda Trent	$3.99	☐
HH #28795	PIECES OF SKY by Marianne Willman	$3.99	☐

Harlequin Promotional Titles

#97122	LINGERING SHADOWS by Penny Jordan	$5.99	☐
	(limited quantities available on certain titles)		

	AMOUNT	$
DEDUCT:	**10% DISCOUNT FOR 2+ BOOKS**	$
	POSTAGE & HANDLING	$
	($1.00 for one book, 50¢ for each additional)	
	APPLICABLE TAXES*	$_____
	TOTAL PAYABLE	$_____
	(check or money order—please do not send cash)	

To order, complete this form and send it, along with a check or money order for the total above, payable to Harlequin Books, to: **In the U.S.:** 3010 Walden Avenue, P.O. Box 9047, Buffalo, NY 14269-9047; **In Canada:** P.O. Box 613, Fort Erie, Ontario, L2A 5X3.

Name: _____

Address:_____ City: _____

State/Prov.: _____ Zip/Postal Code: _____

*New York residents remit applicable sales taxes.
 Canadian residents remit applicable GST and provincial taxes..

HBACK-JS